FOREVERGREEN

James Alan Ross

ISBN: 1543092853
ISBN 13: 9781543092851
Library of Congress Control Number: 2017907650
CreateSpace Independent Publishing Platform, North Charleston, SC

FOREVERGREEN

by

James Alan Ross

For rights inquiries contact:

Sarah Hershman

sara@hershmanrightsmanagement.com

For events, appearances, and media inquiries contact:

forevergreen.book@gmail.com

facebook.com/forevergreen.book

instagram.com/forevergreen.book

Edited by Leslie Bauman

Pine tree artwork by John Bigl

Cover layout by Katherine Gray

info@Kgray.ca   www.Kgray.ca

For Sidney and Jade

Thank you to Leslie Bauman for not being afraid to challenge me and to tell me when something isn't as good as it could be. Your attention to detail brought the most out of every single sentence, turning *Forevergreen* into a better story and me into a better writer. I can't thank you enough for the honesty, insight, and work you put into this project.

Thank you to Lisa Karakaya for your support and professional advice on this project. From early drafts to query letters, your input has always been appreciated and valued.

Thank you to Sarah Hershman for reading an early manuscript and believing in it. Your hard work and dedication is inspiring.

Prologue

Anxious with speculation, she cautiously peered around the corner of the open garage doorway. The beaker above the Bunsen burner on top of the folding table behind her began to violently boil over. She slid her protective goggles down over her brown eyes and pressed the button on the wall to tell the paneled garage door to descend.

Pulling her large, burn proof welding gloves as high as they'd go, she removed the glass bottle from the heat below it. She held it up to the long, yellow light bulb overhead and watched the bubbles dance, as the molecules in the liquid went berserk.

A slammed door from inside the house startled her. Her body jolted from the surprise, as she fought not to spill the concoction. Instantly, she knew her daughter was home from school. The stay-at-home-mother sat the potion down, shook her gloves off, and yanked her white lab coat from her narrow shoulders. The secret could not be revealed this soon.

She knew that. More information and evidence needed to be gathered, analyzed... proven.

She couldn't deny what she had seen, the horrible reality she had stumbled upon while in the pines. Nothing there had made sense; nothing was logical. But, she understood that with the dangers she had witnessed, security and keeping her family safe were imperative. Defeating the Darkness she had discovered, although essential, came second.

"Mom?" Her only child's hungry greeting resonated from inside the vintage two-story. The burnt scent of her research engulfed her, as she abandoned it in the dark.

"I was about to start dinner, Sweetheart," she called out as she entered the kitchen. "I was working in the garage... gardening stuff."

Half of her world stood before her unaware of the imminent threat that lurked in the Village of Lakewood.

The other half was out patrolling the deceptively peaceful streets either unable or unwilling to see the horror that was threatening all that they held dear.

Chapter 1

Monday – 8:04 am

Leaving no doubt that summer was over and fall had arrived, alarm clocks sounded in every bedroom that morning. Kids, carrying new backpacks and wearing posh pieces from their back-to-school shopping sprees, poured from the long line of yellow buses parked by the sidewalk. A mixture of elation and dread swirled in the unseasonably cool air. Smiles and laughter streaked past long faces and dragging feet. Some kids loved this day; others loathed it with distress.

As Iggy looked up at the weathered, metal letters fastened to the high, brick wall, he felt a strong, unfriendly hand grip the back of his neck.

"*Igor*," growled Mike with vigor, and squeezed tightly.

"Owe," Iggy exclaimed in pain. "Dude, knock it off." He squirmed himself free with a turn and a twist.

"You're such a loser," Mike badgered him, proudly.

Iggy rolled his eyes, looked up again at the letters. *Lakewood Pines Middle School.* The letter "I" in *Pines* shaped like a tall, skinny pine tree.

Mike wrapped his arm around Iggy's neck, ruffled his light brown hair, and spoke directly into his ear. "It's 1990, Igor."

"What's your point?" asked Iggy, bothered by Mike's invasive grasp. *Would this kid ever grow up?*

"This is *our* decade," he declared, mischievously. "The first first day of school of the nineties. The decade we'll start high school, graduate high school, go to college, and party with sorority chicks."

Iggy looked at him, wondering why Mike even bothered to speak to him, given their notoriously rancid relationship. "We're starting *seventh grade,*" Iggy stated, hinting that Mike might be getting just a tad carried away with his fantasies of older women.

"Look! There's Liz," Mike signaled by nodding in her direction. "Igor, how could you mess that up? You've got to be a total idiot."

"It's complicated," Iggy answered, desperately watching Liz walk through the school's main entrance without him. He'd have been just fine if Mike had never spoken to him again.

Mike smirked, "My neighbor says even the guys in high school have an eye on her. Dave Jensen actually *called* her a couple weeks ago."

"What?" Iggy's mouth dropped open, amazed by the news. "But, she's –,"

With a touch of evil, Mike laughed. "Better figure it out, *Igor*."

He slapped Iggy on the back, causing him to stumble forward. A few loose papers fell from Iggy's backpack, but he didn't notice. He was watching her. Black curls bounced off her shoulders with each step as Liz strolled through the glass doorway.

It had always been *her*. *Always*.

Giddy chatter echoed through the gymnasium; all

the voices wadded up into a ball and bopped from one wall to the next. Hopes, expectations, and even some crushes renewed today. *Day one*. Broken hearts from the previous year healed, and roving eyes urged Cupid to be generous with his arrows.

Still, everyone kept an eye on Liz and Iggy. Their breakup last year rattled the class, the entire middle school. A version of the story was told across every kitchen table in Lakewood over the summer. Yet, no one really knew what had happened. In fact, it all had happened so fast that Iggy could hardly recall the details. And it's hard to accept something that you don't completely understand.

Feeling numb, helpless, Iggy sat down next to Jeff. *How could I have let this happen?*

He saw Liz, four rows of bleachers in front of him, giggling with her girlfriends. His heart sank hopelessly to the sandy bottom of his soul. He'd been miserable since the breakup happened, and, unbelievably, it appeared that she was doing just fine without him.

She turned to say something to Sara; Iggy could

see the dimple on Liz's delicate cheek. She glanced back, her eyes involuntarily connecting with his. He smiled and prayed she'd return it.

Her eyebrows lifted, slightly, sending a shiver through his entire body. It wasn't a smile, but it was something. He'd take anything he could get.

"Locker partners?" Jeff asked. But, Iggy was in another place, remembering how it felt to hold Liz's soft hand at the football games and in the hallway between classes like nothing else mattered but *them*.

"Hey!" Jeff elbowed Iggy in his ribs. "Locker partners?"

Snapping to, Iggy nodded. "Of course. Are you kidding? You even have to ask?"

"The tradition continues," Jeff said ceremoniously and put up his hand for a high-five. Iggy quickly gave it to him.

Keeping his eyes on Liz, he reminded Jeff, "No stereo this year." Jeff's head dropped theatrically.

"Seriously, we almost got suspended last year for that," Iggy told him. "I don't want to deal with that again."

"Fine," Jeff swiftly recovered from his disenchantment. His mom had been furious about the stereo incident anyway. "Did you watch the video countdown on MTV last night?"

Liz peeped over her shoulder at Iggy again, briefly. He let out a sigh of relief. *She was curious about him, missing him. Maybe?*

Finally looking at Jeff, Iggy replied, "No, I didn't. We were watching America's Funniest Home Videos."

"You gotta' see the dancing in this new video. It's, um, by... I don't remember, but it's awesome!" He made jagged movements with his arms, imitating what he had seen on the television the previous night. "It's like, *weird.*"

Jeff's story was cut short by Principal Warren's voice booming through the P.A. system. "Welcome, Students, to another year at Lakewood Pines Middle School." As their head educator addressed them, the student body's collective voice began to taper off like the fadeout at the end of a song.

"It's always my pleasure to see you all seated here

on the bleachers on the first day of school," he paused. The kids moaned, wishing for just one more day of the summer vacation that seemed to pass by in fast forward.

"Okay, okay," he motioned gingerly with his hands. "Bring it back down. We have said good-bye to last year's seventy-three eighth graders, but today we welcome seventy-seven new fifth graders!"

The sixth, seventh, and eighth graders booed and hissed loudly, while the nervous fifth graders cowered with worry about how they'd be treated now. This type of welcome from their older schoolmates was confirming their worst fears.

"Now, now," Principal Warren nurtured, facing the fifth graders in his expensive designer suit and tie. "Don't let them fool you. They all remember what today was like for them. They'll treat you with respect and kindness." He turned and winked, dramatically, at the three older grades. He put on the same tired act year after year.

They all snickered, until the principal's face became straight, stern. He paused before stepping close to the mic again with his voice subdued.

"Before we go into our usual First Day events, I've been asked to…" He cleared his throat, "I've been asked by the Village Police to make an important announcement." The gym suddenly fell silent.

After a moment, he continued, "A young lady by the name of Sissy Daniels moved into our wonderful school district about four weeks ago. She has been registered to join our outstanding seventh grade class and has been really looking forward to it."

He seemingly choked down a lump that had formed in his throat. "I met her last week. She seemed to be an energetic and nice girl." He looked down at the hardwood floor, before continuing. The students crept to the edge of their seats, wondering where his story was headed. The expensive shoe at the end of his long leg tapped the floor, gently.

"Her parents haven't seen her in the last forty-eight hours." His nose bumped the mic, sending a thud through the gymnasium. It rattled loudly over the gasps and whispers trickling from the anxious audience when he grabbed hold of the tall stand to stabilize it.

"She's missing," he told them, firmly. "If any of you know anything… anything at all, please go to one of your teachers, the guidance counselor, or myself. Her family is very scared and upset. Please remember any information is valuable at this time." Feedback from the speakers buzzed off the ceiling with a dramatic hum.

Looks darted around the gym, and undertones built into a wave of voices that rippled across the sea of worried students. As they stirred, Liz turned, locking troubled eyes with Iggy, and her concerned expression spoke to him. Several nearby conversations nervously morphed into insensitive jokes and snickers with blatant disregard for the girl's safety. Even Jeff seemed to be ill at ease and smirking.

Then, from his right, Iggy heard a distinct roaring. *"Ha. Ha. Ha."*

He whipped his head around to see Mike laughing and slapping hands with the boys from his circle. Annoyed at their immaturity, Iggy grunted in disgust and rolled his eyes before gazing back towards Liz, but her back was now to him. Her forehead almost touched the brown haired girl beside her, and she appeared to be muttering the same displeasure about Mike.

The principal composed himself, peeked to his right out of the gym entrance at the Chief of Police who was standing in the hall. Principal Warren had asked him to stay out of sight of the kids until he had a chance to break the news to them himself.

The principal took a deep, calming breath, turned to the mic and began his annual start-of-the-school-year-speech filled with goofy poems and jokes, acting like he hadn't just made the most disturbing announcement imaginable. Soon, they'd all know their schedules, locker combinations, and if they'd be having lunch break with their closest friends. That was all fine and dandy.

Those are questions they'd been asking all summer. But, for several of them, right then the only questions were, "Who is Sissy Daniels?" And "What happened to her?"

Chapter 2

The morning assembly commotion rapidly dissolved. Students stood chatting and shuffling in locker assignment lines and then wandered loudly to classes. Iggy, Liz, and Mike had been assigned the same homeroom where they would be for first period the entire year; it was with Mr. Miller, Language Arts. Three rows deep, Iggy and Liz sat next to each other based on Mr. Miller's chart. Iggy's heart fluttered and sank. That would either be a blessing or a curse for Iggy, depending on where their relationship went that semester. If there was any relationship at all, that is.

Before Mr. Miller could formally introduce himself, the door of the classroom creaked open, bashfully. A tall, broad, African-American man, dressed in a police uniform quietly entered. The kids all peered at Liz for a moment, but the gun on his hip promptly drew them to the seriousness of the situation.

"I'm Chief Jackson," he announced, removing his hat. "I know that many of you know me through my daughter, Liz. Hi, Sweetheart," he said, looking at her. She nodded, surprised to see her father.

"What your principal mentioned this morning is extremely serious," he explained to the attentive group. "A girl is missing from the village."

"Is she dead?" asked a hollow voice from the back corner of the room.

Chief Jackson lifted his eyes to Jade. Her black leather jacket and shiny combat boots set her apart from the rest of the fashion conformed students. "We are praying that she isn't."

"What happened to her?" she queried, straightening herself from her usual slouch.

"Jade, we don't know," the experienced defender of the law told her, candidly. "But, there are only about twelve-hundred people living here in town-maybe twice that in the total district-and we'll find out if someone took her or harmed her. In fact, we believe that some kids in this school can help us figure that out."

Iggy sat up, noticing Mike staring blankly into his wooden desk. The obnoxious boy hadn't looked at Liz's dad once.

"You're going to see some of us around the school today," Chief Jackson informed. "Don't let us scare you. We may pull some of you aside and ask some questions, so just cooperate with us, please. Thanks, gang." He put his hat on and glared, noticeably, at Mike before leaving the classroom.

Liz noticed Mike, too, and looked at Iggy. Their eyes connected... like they used to. Iggy could see her worries, her fears. Those familiar eyes hadn't changed since kindergarten. He'd seen them reflect every emotion she'd ever had, at one point or another. Even the worst ones. He could read what went on inside of her. She was aware, so she didn't attempt to camouflage it.

Short looks and timid squints were all that anyone exchanged that morning. Students in the halls moved gingerly with an armed officer standing in each one. Almost no one spoke above a whisper and *no one* was late for classes. Even the cafeteria had cops inside, surveying the crowd. The long tables were filled with quiet kids, picking at square pieces of pepperoni pizza and sipping from small cartons of chocolate milk. The normally ruckus room was tranquil, hesitant.

"I think everyone needs to relax a little," boomed Mike's voice through the calm atmosphere about six seats down from Iggy. "I mean, what do I care about some kid gone missing?"

"I agree," Jeff approved, suddenly feeling brave. "She probably just ran away." Giggles fluttered up from the table, like leaves spinning in a cyclone. Jeff couldn't resist the chance to grasp a moment of acceptance from the wild group that spent most days teasing and provoking him.

"What about you, *Igor*?" Mike called, standing up. The group of boys all stared at Iggy, waiting for his reply.

"*Well?*" Mike asked again, forcefully.

Iggy looked up from his plate and saw Liz watching from a table away. "There's a kid missing," he paused. "I think it's pretty serious."

The boys at the table looked to Mike for guidance on how they should react to Iggy's statement of concern. At first, their leader appeared to just stare at Iggy. But Iggy could see a sadistic smile behind his eyes. Within a moment, everyone seated at the table was burst into laughter.

Mike extended his toned arm, pointed his finger at Iggy, and let out a hysterical explosion. "What a wuss!" he bellowed loud enough for everyone to hear. Mike's taunts, however, ceased when a hand touched his shoulder from behind.

It was a police officer. The table fell silent.

"Michael Lawman?" asked the cop.

"Yeah?" Mike snarled, his voice laced with defiance.

"I need you to come with me, please."

"What do you want with *me?*" Mike asked with a grimace.

The officer sternly tugged on his shoulder, prodding him to obey. "I just need you to come with me. Just for a minute."

Mike yanked his shoulder free from the cop's grip. "*FINE!* Just keep your hands off me." He glared at the officer, then at Iggy. He gave his followers one final exaggerated laugh directed at Iggy, while turning to follow the man in the blue suit.

Mocking cheerfully, he let the officer lead him to another room, asserting his lack of care spitefully. He plopped himself, lazily, down into the chair across from Chief Jackson. "What am I doing here, Mr. Jackson?" he complained with attitude, arms folded.

Liz's father put his elbows on the table. "I just want to talk to you, Michael."

The rude adolescent cranked his neck around and saw the other officer standing behind him. The three of them were alone in the teacher's lounge. The scent from a recently used ashtray lingered between Mike and Chief Jackson. Resembling the lightning flashes of an approaching storm, the aging, fluorescent light flickered sporadically above them.

"Are you even allowed to talk to me without my parents here?" Mike harshly objected and folded his arms.

"Would you like me to call your parents, Mike?" the chief asked with his baritone voice, confident that Mike did not want that.

Mike crinkled his eyes, then snarled his response, "No, I don't."

"How are things at home?"

The boy smirked, "Like you don't know."

"Do you know Sissy Daniels?"

That smirk evolved quickly into a shallow laugh. He tipped his neck, pointed his face straight up at the water stained ceiling tiles, and laid his palms flat on the table. "No. I have not a single clue who she even is."

Thump. Thump. Thump.

Chief Jackson, whose stone faced expression hadn't budged, watched Mike's finger tapping against the table.

Thump. Thump. Thump.

It was loud and deliberate, like a metronome, a

ticking clock. The expert interrogator refused to acknowledge it. "You've got quite a reputation around school. Around the whole village, really."

Mike tilted his head forward, a gleam formed in his eyes. He looked at Jackson, with malice. "Did Elizabeth fill your head with rumors about me?"

Thump. Thump. Thump.

His tapping continued. He worked hard to get under the policeman's skin, but the chief continued to ignore the annoying thumping.

"We're not talking about Liz. We are talking about *you*," he said, pointing at the troubled youth.

"What's the matter, Sir? Don't want me to tell you the juicy rumors about your little princess?"

Thump. Thump. Thump.

Mike leaned his body forward, inching closer to Liz's father.

Thump. Thump. Thump.

"You spend much time in the woods? Behind the school?" wondered Chief Jackson.

Mike smiled. *Thump. Thump. Thump.* "You mean

the pines?"

"Yes, the pines."

"Nope," Mike laughed again.

Thump. Thump. Thump.

"Get him outta' here," Jackson ordered the officer that had brought him in. Mike winked and stood up, feeling accomplished.

Once the boy exited the lounge, Jackson let out a sigh. "Tell Principal Warren to make an announcement," he told the other officer. "No one under eighteen is allowed out of their residence after the sun goes down. Until further notice."

"What about the high school football game this Friday?" the officer questioned.

"Reschedule it for Saturday afternoon," the Chief of Police instructed. "Any minor found outside at night will have a mark on their permanent record. And they'll have *me* to deal with."

*

One year ago…

She walked past the kids that filled the tables and those lined up behind the arcade games into the open kitchen. The shop owner rolled large, thin circles of pizza dough out on the flour coated counter. He glanced at her and met her eyes momentarily, before she closed the door of the backroom office behind her.

He tilted his head towards the noisy students, holding his ear to them, listening. Every ounce of information, every clue he could gather could be vital to the cause and could be the missing piece that might blow their investigation wide open. He always kept an ear and an eye open.

All the kids knew the pines had secrets; they all gossiped and murmured about what they've heard their parents, siblings discuss and speculate about the evergreens. Blurred by rumors and unsubstantiated claims, the pines were an epic legacy. Claims that he and the woman in his office aimed to prove true.

After closing the office door, she pressed her date

of birth into the keypad on the small safe that hid under the shop owner's desk. From her purse, she pulled a stack of Polaroid photos. Flipping through the thick and white bordered images, she shook her head.

Every creak that the old floor and walls made caused her to flinch.

Nervously, she sealed them away, locked in the fireproof box, and stood to peer out through the dust covered window. In the alleyway she could see a tall, lanky, well-dressed man slipping around the corner of the brick building and out of sight. She put her hand to her mouth, closed her eyes, and took a long inhale, holding it briefly.

It had to be him, she thought…

Chapter 3

Monday – 11:02 pm

Changing out of her cozy pajamas into the jeans and sweatshirt she had taken off hours earlier, Liz peered out of her bedroom window. Hesitating, she looked at her bedroom door. Her father believed she was tucked under her covers, ready to sleep for the night, safe.

She slid the window open, quietly reached for the longest branch that extended out of the giant maple tree in the front yard. She dropped from there to another limb, to the trunk, and slithered down. Some sticking to her fleece, shards of bark flicked off from the tree trunk.

"Practice makes perfect," whispered Liz to herself.

She brushed herself clean, bent down to tighten her shoe laces. Windy and colder than it should be, darker than she expected, Liz pulled her hood over her head, cinched the strings tight, and walked into the night. She knew with certainty she may end up regretting it.

*

Iggy's feet dangled to the sand under the rusty swing set. Questioning his judgment on that night, he rocked back and forth. Fear of getting caught on a late night rendezvous always existed, but now Iggy was in direct defiance of a police ordinance and that fear was magnified. All that considered, the sound of mischievous feet crunching the grass from behind didn't startle him.

Instead, it gave him hope.

He knew the tempo of Liz's walk by heart. Her steps played the sort of tune Iggy and Liz slow danced to at the school dance last spring. He didn't turn toward her but waited for her to sit in the swing next to him, like she always had.

She didn't acknowledge him either. She just swayed, catching her breath.

Leaves on the trees rustled in the growing breeze all around them. Turning yellow, red, and orange much sooner than normal, some leaves had even already fluttered to the ground. He could relate to those few leaves that tumbled scared down the sidewalk, carried away from the only thing that had ever made them feel safe.

Iggy remembered meeting up with Liz here last September and being surrounded by lush, green leaves still firmly attached to the trees that birthed them. He found it curious, but weather patterns were the furthest thing from his mind. Pleading his case to her, defending his innocence is what consumed him.

He couldn't have cared less what color the leaves were.

Iggy turned and could see the soft lines of her face. The light musky perfume that she always gently applied to her neck floated to him, and he swallowed the urge to reach for her hand. The moonlight created a glow around her that nearly hypnotized him. Her beauty spoke to him in a whisper he could hardly hear over the harsh voice of logic that suddenly erupted.

"Why didn't you call me?" he asked, unable to mask the pain he carried.

She twisted her swing in an arch rhythmically and, just for a split second, peeked at him from under her long eyelashes. "I didn't know about any of this, Iggy. All this surprised to me, too. I found out at school, just like you did."

"Not about the girl," he shook his head. "I left you a dozen messages, even a letter. You never answered." Iggy turned his face away from Liz and somberly gazed at the eavesdropping moon.

"When did you get back from Detroit?" He tried to keep the desperation inside from leaking through his voice.

"Last week," she told him, timidly, trying to avoid the inevitable reality of having to face their breakup.

"You spent the whole summer at your grandma's and didn't even call when you got home," Iggy could no longer hide his misery. "I wanted to see you. We haven't even spoken since you left."

"My dad -,"

"Your *dad*?!" Iggy whispered, loudly, "What does your dad even have to do with -,"

"Iggy!" she interrupted him.

He ignored her. "Your dad has always liked me. Until *now*? Besides, are you going to let him come between us?"

She sat quiet, shaking her head. She kept her voice low, "Iggy, we've been going together, been boyfriend and girlfriend, or whatever you want to call it, since kindergarten, but… it's what happened last year in sixth grade. And it's not just my dad."

Her throat began to swell. She swallowed the lump that formed there, and kept her composure. "It's me, too."

Iggy's heart raced. "I *didn't* start that rumor, Liz."

She looked at the boy who had been her closest friend for as long as she could remember. "I hope not," she said, delicately.

They shared the silence, the wonder, the uncertainty. It wasn't supposed to be this way. Not between them. Their hands gripped the chilly chain ropes that held the swings in the cold night as they swayed back and forth.

After several minutes, Liz gave in first, "We shouldn't be out here, Iggy."

"Then why *are* we? Why did you come?"

She looked at him, directly, "I wanted to see you. I've missed you."

Her words were huge to him, intoxicating. He refused to relax, though. Just because she missed him, didn't mean she… still loved him. "How many times have we met here on these swings in the middle of the night?"

She smiled, remembering the moments they've shared here. Specifically, their first kiss, under the stars with small drops of rain falling against her cheek. "Dozens. Hundreds. Millions!" she laughed, only to have her heart stop when she spied the yellow beams of headlights, rounding the corner in front of them.

They both jumped from their swings and rushed over to the spiral slide. Liz hid behind it entirely, while Iggy kept his eyes where he could see the vehicle pass by.

"Patrol car?" she asked.

"Yeah," he confirmed, still watching.

"Let's get home, Iggy," she said, moving out from behind the structure.

"Wait!" he whispered loudly, holding his hand up. "I see someone walking."

Staying behind him, she peeked her head around his shoulder. "Who is it?" she wondered.

He mouthed the name *Mike* to her, then watched as the dark figure moved in and out of sight under the street lights.

Mike seemed alert, ready to pounce into the bushes, or behind a tree if another patrol car came by. The wind twitching at each branch made him jumpy. He moved slow, feet dragging, looking around for another car. Or maybe looking for someone else? Someone he was expecting?

Liz and Iggy watched him cross Fourth Street, stopping at the large, green dumpster in the bank's parking lot. He peered in every direction, then at his watch. He leaned against the metal dumpster, on edge.

"What's he doing?" Liz whispered, close to Iggy's ear.

Feeling her breath against his ear sent a shiver down his spine. He played it cool. "I think he's waiting for someone."

Mike checked his watch again, then his eyes stared straight down Main Street. Headlights, although from quite a distance, illuminated his face. He turned to run, but suddenly stopped himself. He took one more glance at his watch, then looked again towards the approaching vehicle, holding off panic. Quickly, he reached deep into the front pocket of his blue jeans and removed an object. He held it out in front of him, taking a final look at it.

Iggy and Liz watched as the headlights reflected off the long, thin, gold necklace in Mike's hand. It shimmered brightly against the dark night. There was a large pendant on it, but from where they crouched, Iggy and Liz couldn't decipher its shape.

Mike lifted the heavy lid of the dumpster, hurled the necklace inside and bolted behind the brick building that was Lakewood Village Bank.

Liz stooped behind the slide, and Iggy did the same. The patrol car slowly pulled up to the dumpster and stopped. Letting the car run, the officer stepped out, shined his light around where he certainly had caught a glimpse of Mike. Iggy popped his head out to check on the situation, but when he did, he put his face right into the officer's flashlight beam. He'd been spotted!

"Hey!" yelled the cop, beginning to run towards them.

"What happened?" Liz cried, her heart pounding.

"You wait here! I'll run and get him to chase me. When he's not looking, get out of here and back to your house." Iggy coached her, a hand on each of her shoulders, holding her straight in front of him.

"Are you sure?" she asked, worrying. "What if he catches you?"

"He won't. I promise." Iggy sounded more confident than he really was. "I'll see you at school tomorrow!"

He looked deep into her eyes, then briskly turned

away. He lunged out from behind the slide, the officer's light on his back, and sprinted across the playground. Liz watched the cop, tailing Iggy, and slowly snuck off in the other direction. She wanted to look back, but resisted. She trusted Iggy's promise that he wouldn't be captured.

"Stop!" the hefty officer screamed, repeatedly. "Stop!"

Iggy didn't listen. He couldn't. If Liz's father had a problem with him over the summer, imagine if he was captured here. He ran as fast as he could, weaving between the swings and monkey bars. His adrenaline boosted his speed to new, never before reached heights. He leapt over the seesaw, lengthening the gap between him and his pursuer.

The pudgy officer was unable to make the jump and lost ground when he was forced to go around the obstacle. When Iggy finally reached the sidewalk, the rubber tread on his sneakers gripped the concrete, bolstering him into overdrive. The officer had no chance now and knew it. He ceased his chase and hollered a few more hopeless times at the fleeing boy. *Stop! Stop! Stop running!*

Iggy was gone. Home free.

Chapter 4

Tuesday – 8:10 am

As the bell signaling the start of the day rang loudly, rain fell heavily outside the window of Mr. Miller's classroom. Students pulled at their damp clothes and combed through their wettish hair after their walk into the building. The notion to carry an umbrella never crossed the minds of twelve year olds.

Thunder rolled over the school behind gray clouds, as Iggy watched the tall pine trees outside stormily dance. The thick pine forest covered a large portion of the school property and far beyond, mostly in the rear and just past the Little League fields.

Older students often told alarming tales about the shadowed pines that younger kids never knew whether or not to believe. Even many of the adults in Lakewood refused to dispel the farfetched yet somehow believable rumors.

Whatever *was* true, the pines had a long history in the village - a mysterious one. The green, prickly evergreens stretched with despair for what seemed like forever into the distance. An endless mass of green.

Liz took her seat next to Iggy, her black hair glistening from the raindrops that stubbornly clung to each strand. He wanted to stare at her until she turned his gaze, but he fought the urge. To build on the tiny bit of progress he made last night is what he needed to do. Staring like an obsessed stalker would only set him further back.

Mr. Miller's voice battled with the sound of rain pelting against the windows. "I expect you to be in your seats when that bell rings," he bellowed, with authority.

The kids scurried to their desks. No one wanted to be Mr. Miller's early year discipline example.

Jade rushed past Mike's desk with an awkward strut, quickly sliding a folded sheet of paper into his textbook. He pretended as though he didn't notice her, making an attempt to keep any attention from the cagey girl.

Iggy and Liz simultaneously looked at each other, having both seen what Jade had just done. The tall, skinny girl scooted swiftly to the back of the room and was the last student to reach her seat.

When Mr. Miller began taking attendance by calling each student's name out loud, Mike casually pulled the paper from between the pages of his book.

"Igor Andrews?" Mr. Miller called, stridently.

"Here," Iggy replied, eyes glued to the paper in Mike's hand.

Mr. Miller continued down the list, while Mike calmly unfolded the paper. Liz, two seats directly behind Mike, didn't have a great viewpoint. She reached across the aisle, slapped Iggy's arm, wondering if he could see better from his seat. Iggy stretched his neck.

"Elizabeth Jackson?" yelled Mr. Miller, still competing with the deafening rain.

"Here," she answered, waiting for Iggy to respond to her cuff.

He shook his head, unable to get a clear look at what is written on the sheet.

"Michael Lawman?" said Mr. Miller.

"Here," Mike mumbled without looking up, concentrating on the note from Jade. He took out his pencil and scribbled something on to it. When he finished, he folded it up and placed it back under the front cover of his textbook, inconspicuously. Iggy looked at Liz and shrugged his shoulders, letting her know that he couldn't see any of the writing.

"Jade Wilson?" Mr. Miller finally called, finishing the list of names.

"Here," she called back to him from the last row of desks mimicking the teacher's own voice.

Before Mr. Miller could look up from his attendance log, the classroom door opened. A police officer entered, carrying a large sheet of paper and a small box of thumb tacks. He walked over, quietly, to the cork slab on the wall to the right of the chalkboard. Without saying anything, he hung the poster up perfectly straight with a red tack in each corner. It was huge with bright colors.

It was a picture of a girl, fine, black hair, with a carefree smile. She was wearing a t-shirt and a shimmering, gold necklace with a large pendant shaped like a dove hanging on it.

Above her, written in all capital, black letters, was one word - *MISSING*.

Liz and Iggy turned to each other, knowing their unspoken suspicions may have some merit. Somehow, they needed to get their hands on that note inside of Mike's book and read it. The necklace in the girl's picture looked an awful lot like the one they saw Mike toss away last night and that note from Jade to Mike just might just confirm that it was.

Sitting through class under those circumstances was complete torture. Mr. Miller droned on about what he expected this year, what he'd be teaching. He commented on the unusually cold weather several times, then ironically verbally reprimanded the students if he caught them staring out the window at the dark, threatening clouds.

It was impossible to look at Mr. Miller during his lecture without seeing Sissy Daniels' face on the poster, so most of the kids didn't. They all just kept their faces buried in their textbooks. It was a horrific thought, where she might be. To see her smiling face gazing back at them, knowing that whatever happened was bad, was chilling.

The clock ticked slower than Iggy ever thought was possible. As soon as the bell sounded at the end of first period, Liz spun herself to face him.

"We have to get that note," she whispered, under the commotion of everyone shuffling their items to head to their next class.

Iggy nodded, knowing that he had Physical Education with Mike next down in the gym. Funneling into the halls, kids from every direction were stunned and bewildered. Posters with Sissy Daniels' face on them hung throughout the halls.

Overwhelmed students, stopped and gawked, as the disturbance of their safe, quiet lives become more real, more frightening. Every ten feet was another poster, the same cheerful face, over and over. This was really happening. A kid from Lakewood Village was gone, vanished without a trace. Groups of kids gathered in front of the pictures, speechless. No one had to say anything.

They all felt the same – scared.

Liz grabbed Iggy's elbow from behind. "Look," she said. They watched, through an immobile crowd as Jade, nonchalantly, took the note back from Mike. "Don't worry, I have her in Study Hall next," Liz informed Iggy and headed down the hall following the peculiar girl.

Iggy gazed at Liz, his favorite person, walking away. He was scared, too about Sissy Daniels like everyone. But he was more worried about losing Liz. He was holding on to her, what they used to have, with his fingertips hoping she didn't slip away.

Before Liz turned the corner to her Study Hall, she looked back at Iggy for just a moment.

His heart melted.

*

"Well, we won't be starting baseball today," declared a

disappointed Mr. Armstrong. "It's raining cats and dogs out there."

The gym teacher wore his socks high and his shorts even higher. His skin-tight t-shirt, with the word *Coach* printed across his chest, formed around his muscular body. He blew the whistle that always hung around his neck as hard as he could, sending a screech echoing through the gymnasium.

"Dodgeball!" he thunderously yelled, creating a frenzy among the second period boys. They all cheered and ran, placing their backs against the folded up bleachers in a perfectly formed row.

Mr. Armstrong strolled down the line of kids, awkwardly examining them, sizing them up. "Lawman, you're a captain," he said to Mike. "And, Andrews you're the other captain," he told Iggy.

"Great, boys against girls!" Mike mocked, to unabashed laughing. Even Mr. Armstrong found it comical and didn't hide his joy.

At Lakewood Pines Middle School, respect was earned and lost on the dodgeball court. The competition was always fierce, and the stakes were high. Legacies were written on the court, where a kid's life could change for the better, or worse.

Iggy and Mike had undeniably been the best players in their grade since elementary school, but Mike had always been able to get the best of Iggy. Always on opposing teams, Mike continuously pulled out the victory. He'd always been a bit bigger, faster and, most importantly, luckier. Iggy hoped that in seventh grade, he could change that.

The two boys took turns choosing which classmates would be on their respective teams. Back and forth, they made their selections. Each of Iggy's picks drew a snide look or comment from Mike, as though he was building a weak team that stood little chance at winning. When the last boy was picked, the teams were set.

Game time.

The two groups each took their positions on either side of the gym, studying their opponents, calculating strategy. Mr. Armstrong placed five air filled, rubber balls along the centerline of the court. It served as an invisible wall, a boundary, that could not be crossed, or the perpetrator was ejected from play. Players on each squad focused on a ball and believed they had the best shot at getting to it before someone from the other team.

Heels against the wall, they all leaned in. One foot forward, arms positioned to race. Mr. Armstrong stood on the sideline, out of bounds at the equator of the battlefield. He raised his arm straight up in the air, slowly put his metal whistle between his lips, and curtly blew the start.

*

Ms. Cain peeled back the foil lid on her yogurt cup, slid her plastic spork between her lips, and wiped the creamy substance clean off. "Mmm," she moaned. "There's nothing like yogurt. All my life I've never found anything like yogurt." The kids watched her gaze up at the ceiling.

"Raspberry, blackberry. Those two are the best. Oh, and strawberry."

She behaved much older than she was. Dressed

older, too. The students paid little attention to the portly woman's narrative. It was Study Hall, a laid-back environment. None of them cared about the love affair she was having with the dairy product.

"Can you believe how cold it's been?" she asked the kids. Not one of them answered her.

"Can you imagine if it was winter all the time? All the trees with no leaves, just standing out there naked. Well, except our pines, that is. I swear that nothing is more powerful than the sight of an evergreen tree in the dead of winter. While all other things fade, it remains in its glory."

"How was your summer?" Liz asked Jade, interrupting her doodling. The two were seated next to each other, front row.

Slowly looking up from her notebook, Jade replied, "Fine. I guess." She focused back down at the page, starting to draw again.

"How was yours?" she asked, not actually caring.

"Good. I was at my grandma's for most of it," Liz said.

"I heard," Jade stated. Her voice was very bland, monotone. She always sounded that way. "I saw Iggy a few times at Greasy's."

Liz smiled. "Greasy's sounds so good. I didn't have pizza one time all summer."

"That kid has been a wreck, since you broke up," Jade said, still drawing.

The thunder had let up, but the rain hadn't. It was pouring down, like buckets. Liz stayed quiet for a moment, not wanting to discuss her and Iggy's break up. Especially with Jade. She changed the subject, "What are you drawing?"

"Trees," replied Jade. "The pines behind the school."

Liz stared at the smudged pencil lead on Jade's paper. "Are those *eyes* you're drawing on the trees?"

"The pines are always watching us, Lizard," Jade informed her, while looking out the window at the woods. "Do you spend much time out there?"

Liz just shook her head, saying nothing. She hated it when Jade called her *Lizard*.

Jade smiled, eerily, and looked back down, continuing her work.

"What's the little one for?" Liz wondered out loud.

Jade peeked at her, not raising her head, "The little tree?"

"Yeah, the one you drew, right in the middle."

"You don't want to know what the little tree is, Lizard," she explained icily.

Liz could see the corner of the note Mike passed back to Jade, sticking out of her book. She needed to get it. "Did you see Mike over the summer?"

Jade turned to her, laughing, "Mike Lawman?"

Her face wrinkled, "Oh my God, I think Mike Lawman kisses his reflection every morning in the mirror. You really think that I would have any reason to see Mike Lawman outside of school? Are you crazy?"

*

The wooden pellet inside Mr. Armstrong's

whistle fluttered erratically, sending a vibration-filled screech across the gym. *It's on!*

Players from both sides charged the centerline, racing towards the rubber balls, and stepping carefully not to accidentally cross the imaginary barrier. Those that arrived first, scooped one up, heaving it towards the other team.

This game was ugly.

Balls pelted boys, and bodies flew everywhere. Timmy Thompson took one in the knee that tripped him, and sent him to the hardwood floor with a bang. Causing him to gasp, Daman Reddy took a forceful blow to the gut. Daman's face turned red as he hunched over and scooted to the sideline, courageously containing his barf and swallowing it back down. Casualties were many.

The start of dodgeball games was always dangerous. The first attacks were all at close range which magnified the wounds. Mike grabbed the ball that bounced back to him off of Daman's belly and sent a fastball right between the eyes of David Garcia, knocking him unconscious.

Mr. Armstrong rushed out, avoiding being drilled himself, and dragged David's limp body out of bounds to safety.

"Great throw!" he yelled to Mike, showing thumbs up, while David laid there, motionless, with the rest of the kids who fell victim to the game's violent beginning.

If a boy was hit by a ball or had a ball he threw get caught, he was out and had to leave the court. Iggy's team had taken an early beating at the centerline, quickly losing over half their players. Mike's team had some losses as well, but had a higher number of players remaining in the game.

The advantage had quickly become Mike's, and Iggy knew it. Iggy took a quick stock of who he had left, shouted inspiring phrases, like - *Don't give up! We're still in this! It's not over 'till it's over!* Jeff nodded, admiring Iggy's tenacity, unwillingness to throw in the towel.

Iggy was a fighter; Mike knew it.

So did Liz.

*

Liz looked at the pencil in Jade's hand and got an idea. She opened her notebook and started to scribble. She wasn't really drawing, just making circles, lines, and other shapes. Then she pressed down, firmly, on the paper, her knuckles clenched. She pushed until the lead snapped off the end of her pencil.

"Oops," Liz said, as she stood up, walked to the pencil sharpener at the front of the classroom, and turned the handle until her pencil was once again sharp and pointy. She took a breath then started the walk back to her seat, preparing to execute her plan. As she turned around the front of her desk, Liz banged her hip into Jade's desk, knocking most of her things down onto the floor.

"Hey, watch it, Lizard!" Jade groaned, annoyed.

"Oh, I'm so sorry!" Liz apologized, "Let me get that for you." She bent down, sifting through the scattered papers.

"I can get it," Jade insisted defensively, dropping down to her knees, pushing Liz out of her way.

Liz just slid back on her knees, "I'm really sorry, Jade."

"Whatever," Jade let out a long exhale. "Just forget about it... my little green Lizard," she hissed, knowing how much it would bother Liz to hear that. Jade slammed her books and papers onto her desktop and went back to her drawing. The sound of falling rain still dominated the room.

Liz raised her hand, casually.

"Elizabeth?" acknowledged Ms. Cain, looking up from the papers she was reviewing at her desk. "What is it, Darling?"

"Ms. Cain, can I use the restroom?"

"Sure, Dear. Just don't linger around the halls. Class is almost over, so why not take your things with you?" Ms. Cain suggested.

Liz stood up, gathered her belongings, and briskly left the room. When she entered the hall, she reached into her back pocket and pulled out a piece of folded paper.

She got it!

She was able to sneak the letter out of the fallen book before Jade could stop her. Better yet, Jade had no idea that she had snagged it.

Resisting the urge to hurry, she moved slowly down the hallway, unable to avoid seeing Sissy Daniels' picture every ten or fifteen feet. Officers were still present, too. One at each end of every hallway eerily. The pictures. The police. Lakewood Pines had never even had Hall Monitors. Now they have this?

She just stayed calm as she turned left at the library and passed the girls restroom. She passed her locker, the cafeteria, even a second set of restrooms. The policemen all recognized her, knowing who she was. She kept walking, moving steadily, at a quick but not alarming pace. She didn't stop once until she reached the gymnasium door.

*

Now in the lead, Iggy's team had made a remarkable comeback. Iggy and Jeff remained on their side, both with a ball in hand. Mike, the lone player left on his side, held two of the rubber balls. The fifth ball was behind him, against the wall, where Iggy and Jeff couldn't get to it.

It was a standoff.

At certain intervals of the game, Mr. Armstrong had blown his whistle, signaling a shift in the centerline. Each time he blew it, the court was shortened up. Now, Mike had just about fifteen feet of the court left, Iggy and Jeff had him literally pinned against the wall.

Mike was beaten, and he knew it. His face appeared panicked as he looked left and right searching for a way to escape defeat. His eyes darted hopelessly for a stray ball; his shoulders dropped succumbing to defeat. Jeff and Iggy surrounded him, without crossing the line, using the back wall as a third member of their team.

"On three!" Iggy yelled to Jeff.

"I'll go high," Jeff noted, confirming he understood Iggy's plan. It was classic dodgeball strategy.

On the count of three they would both throw their ball at Mike. The throws needed to be accurate or Mike could still win. If he was able to deflect Iggy's ball with his ball and Jeff missed, that would leave Iggy and Jeff without any balls and Mike with all of them. Jeff planned to throw high; Iggy would throw low. But they both must hit their target or Mike could escape the attack.

"One, two, three!" Iggy pulled back to throw.

Thinking fast, Mike also threw on three, hit Jeff in the shoulder before he could even release his ball, and knocked Jeff out of the game. He also was quick enough to skip over Iggy's throw, now leaving himself in control of the match. He grabbed a ball in each hand and sprinted down the court after Iggy; the tables had unexpectedly turned. Iggy was against his wall, and Mike's boundary line was now only fifteen feet in front of him.

"You're dead now!" yelled Mike, cocking his arm back, ready to fire. "*Dead!*"

Iggy tried to stay calm, preparing himself for the throw. If he could catch it, he would win. If he was hit, he would lose. Mike launched the first ball at Iggy's feet. Iggy jumped, just in time for it to pass under him. It hit the wall and rolled back to Mike's area. If that was where Mike was going to target, catching the ball will be impossible. His only option was to dodge it. After all, that was the name of the game. Mike prepared his next throw, staring powerfully at Iggy.

"Come on! Throw it!" Iggy yelled. "What are you waiting for?"

Mike just stared. All the students who had been knocked out of the game were screaming. Some for Iggy, and the rest for Mike. They all cheered and clapped for their team captains.

"Throw it!" Iggy yelled again, hoping he could avoid being hit. What was Mike waiting for?

Suddenly, Iggy felt Mike was not looking at him at all, but something behind him instead. Iggy waited. Mike still didn't throw. Mike's eyes were glossed over, like he was somewhere else other than the gym.

Iggy turned and checked over his shoulder. He saw one of the Sissy Daniels posters with her happy face on it, hanging on the wall behind him. Mike's eyes were glued to the girl's dark eyes and gentle grin.

Suddenly, when Iggy looked back to the court, Mike had just let go of the ball. It whizzed past Iggy's ear, hitting Sissy's picture directly. The ball bounced back, landing at Iggy's feet. He scooped it up, knowing that he had Mike off guard. At that point in the game, Iggy could run right up and tag him, since the court lines had shifted to both sides so drastically. Seeing Mike still staring at the poster, paying no attention to him, Iggy decided to throw it.

Iggy reared back, aimed at the center of Mike's chest. It could be the fatal blow, the end of the game, a changing of the guard in the world of dodgeball.

Ready to claim victory, Iggy saw the door at the far end of the gym open from the corner of his eye. Liz walked in and held up the letter for him to see. *She did it.* She was able to get it!

He looked back at Mike, but it was too late. Iggy couldn't even see him anymore. All he could see was a big, red, rubber ball a foot from his face about to collide with it. When it hit him in the forehead, Iggy dropped to the ground. The kids from Iggy's team moaned with disappointment, while the kids on Mike's celebrated their leader's last second heroics. The game was over.

Mike won. Iggy lost. Again.

Mike's team rushed the floor, surrounding him and jumping around enjoying their victory, ecstatically. Iggy didn't even care. He ignored his near concussion and forced his wobbly legs to run to Liz. A large red mark formed on the front of his forehead. It was sore, but he didn't offer it any attention.

"Are you okay?" she worried, touching the swollen blotch.

"I'm fine," he asserted, his sweat collecting on her palm.

"I got it," she bragged, her beautiful smile beaming.

Iggy loved that smile. "What does it say?"

"I didn't read it yet. I was waiting for you," she told him as the sound of Mike's team celebrating floated over to them from the far side of the gymnasium.

Iggy got a chill through his arm when their hands touch for a second, as she handed him the paper. He opened it, so they both could see. At the top of the page was Jade's handwriting.

Sorry, I couldn't meet you. My parents had me under heavy surveillance. Maybe tonight. Clock is ticking...

Under her writing was the part that Mike wrote back to her.

It's okay. I ditched the necklace. Tonight is too risky. Let's meet early. 5:30 tomorrow morning.

Iggy and Liz both slowly lifted their eyes from the note and locked in a stare. They didn't have to verbalize it; they both were thinking it.

What in the world are those two up to?

*

One year ago...

She kneeled and ran her fingers along the soil. The pizza shop owner leaned and looked over her shoulder at the shape pressed in the ground. "Do you think...?" she asked.

"It's a' them," he said nodding. "I a' knew it."

She stood up, put her hands on her hips, gazing up at the branches. "They're active again. Like when Iggy's mom and dad died."

"I saw the light, from a' my window," he looked straight up and pointed. "Clear to the heavens, it a' went."

"A signal? For more to come?"

"Perhaps," he told her. "The atmosphere, their actions, are a' changing. They're movements becoming less predictable. More a' strange each day."

She looked down at the bizarre compression in the dirt again. "They're big. These... things, they're huge."

He pulled a plastic bag from his backpack, began gathering pine needles out of the imprint. She reached down to help, her diamond wedding ring glimmered in the rays of sun that crept through the canopy of pine trees. He saw it shining and grabbed her wrist.

"Any luck with him?" he asked, motioning towards the ring with his unsettled eyes.

She bit her bottom lip, shook her head. "He won't listen. He's scared."

"They're in danger! All of them!" he whispered, violently.

"I know," she held in her emotions. "I know."

"We need him to help us! To keep a' the kids safe. Safe from these tyrants!"

"I just need more time, more proof," she remained hopeful her husband would soon come to grips and accept what was undoubtedly happening in Lakewood. In the pines.

"We are a' running out of time…" he told her, trying not to push her, but being firm, nonetheless.

"Okay," she whispered, unsure. "I'll try again."

"Did you at least give him the axe?"

"I did."

"Did you explain it to him?"

"No," she hung her head. "He already thinks I've lost my mind."

Chapter 5

A large crowd of students formed at the back exit of the school. Most were gathered just inside the doors, keeping themselves out of the lightly falling rain. Hearing murmurs and rumblings from every direction, Iggy and Liz pushed their way through the multitude until they joined those standing outside. Some of the kids joked, not appreciating the tragic circumstances; others stood completely silent. For some, the seriousness had sunk in, as tears dripped down their cheeks.

When Iggy finally got a clear visual of what was attracting all the rubberneckers, he was taken aback. He and Liz let the rain fall on them, speechless, as they watched what was unfolding.

Several police officers, at least six, covered head to toe in dark blue rain gear moseyed around the edges of the pines. Three of them had search dogs on leashes, aggressively sniffing the ground.

The weight of the last two days was collapsing down on everyone. The announcement, the curfew, the posters, now this. What had happened to their school? Their town? This girl named Sissy? It was an awful feeling to imagine what might have happened to her.

Something horrible.

A border of yellow police tape, reading *DO NOT CROSS* was set up, separating the school grounds from the pines. The gray clouds in the darkening sky composed the physical manifestation of the student's collective countenance. The mood hung dark and daunting.

"We have to get to the bank and look in that dumpster," Iggy declared determinedly as he stared at the search team.

"What if it's the same necklace that girl is wearing in that picture?" Liz asked with a tinge of uncertainty.

"Then we tell your dad. If it's that necklace, then Mike and maybe even Jade probably know what happened to her." Seeing Jade lingering not far off from where they stood, Iggy made sure to keep his voice low. The thin and frail girl held her books in front of her, staring concerned at the pines.

"You don't think they could've…" Liz's voice trailed off.

"I don't know, Liz. It's possible," he warned. "Let's get going."

"My dad told me I have to come straight home after school," she said, grabbing his arm. "He's afraid. Not sure if whoever did this to that girl might strike again. Wants me to check in."

"Okay," he studied her hand, clutching him. "I'll go. We'll meet up later."

"Greasy's," she suggested. "I'll meet you there at 4:15."

"What about your dad?"

"I'll get out," she assured him. "I'll sneak, if I have to."

Iggy's long walk to the bank was less than enjoyable. The rain soaked his hair and clothes; the wet grass and puddles on the uneven sidewalks drenched his feet, through the sneakers and socks to his skin. Passing the search party, he witnessed dozens of townsfolk watching from the street and surrounding lawns.

They stared, wondering what could've happened to that poor girl, Sissy Daniels.

Lakewood had never had an abduction, at least on record anyway. Citizens were worried about a possible kidnapper being on the loose, waiting in the bushes, biding time before finding another victim. They worried that Sissy Daniels might be tied up in their neighbor's basement, and the way people were treating each other was proof of their suspicions.

Their eyes said it all. Suddenly, trust wasn't so easily granted. Families who had never locked their front doors when running to the supermarket, now locked all doors and windows.

Iggy had a feeling though that these precautions were unnecessary. He didn't believe Sissy was taken; he thought something was *done* to her. Something horrific. Killed even. Finding that necklace was imperative.

Traffic streamed down Main Street and customers still shuffled in and out of the bank. Getting into the dumpster without causing a scene seemed impossible. By the time Iggy got close enough to peek inside the open lid, it no longer mattered.

It was empty. Well, almost empty.

All he found were a few flattened, grease stained pizza boxes sitting on the bottom. The garbage men must have emptied the dumpsters during school. Just the stench of rotten food still filled the metal container. He held his breath, defending against the smell, and scanned the area one last time for the necklace.

Nothing.

His chance at seeing if the necklace Mike tossed away was the same one that Sissy was wearing in the poster was gone.

*

"Where are you headed?" Chief Jackson said to his tip-toeing daughter. He was dressed in his uniform and was slipping his rain gear on over it.

Halting in her tracks, Liz tried acting as though she wasn't sneaking through the living room to the back door. "Just heading to Greasy's, Dad," she told him with a smile.

"I don't think I want you out there today with all that's going on. Besides, it's raining," he said tugging at his raincoat.

"But, Dad, I'm craving Greasy's. I've been gone all summer." She tried using her *I'm-your-only-daughter* eyes.

"I'll order some and pick it up for you. I can do that before I head to the pines," he offered. "Can you hand me the phone? Is the number still on speed dial?"

Her soft, persuasive eyes turned defiant, "Dad! I want to see my friends." Knowing she stood little chance at coaxing him, Liz reluctantly handed him the phone.

"You mean Iggy?" He protectively peered at her and pressed *Speed Dial 7.* Liz's summer had been a mood, touchy one after her break up with Iggy, and he didn't want a rekindling of her gloom and irritability.

"Yes, Giuseppe. I want to order a large pepperoni," he said to the man on the other end of the line. "Pick up... Yeah, you know who it is... Twenty minutes? Okay, thank you." He hung up, pushed down the antenna on the cordless receiver.

"You mean you want to see Iggy?" he repeated.

"Dad..." she began, not wanting to have that discussion again. The one where she defended Iggy, but then had to explain why she broke up with him in the next breath.

"You know, we had an officer spot a juvenile out late last night. He even chased him on foot," he told her with an austere expression.

Liz kept her eyes low and occupied as she picked a hangnail off her pinky.

"We have a pretty good idea who it was." He zipped up his long, blue coat with Lakewood Village Police embroidered over his heart.

"You do?"

"Yup," he nodded with confidence. "We think we know *exactly* who it was."

Her eyes lifted to see her father's face. "You think it was *Mike?* I mean, maybe it was Mike?"

"It was dark when he chased him, but the officer got a decent look at another boy in the headlights just a minute earlier. We'll be reviewing the footage from the dash-cam soon. I hope my suspicions are wrong."

"What are your suspicions, Dad?" she asks him with a flare on *Dad.*

"Some of those boys at school are trouble, Liz. Watch yourself around them," he advised her. "Mike Lawman. Iggy."

"Iggy? Are you serious?" her tone became increasingly tense.

"Iggy is with that boy a lot. Too much. I think, maybe, Iggy is becoming a little too much like Mike."

"No, Dad, Iggy doesn't really get along with Mike."

"I'm not so sure about that. I've seen them together at games and parties. Didn't they do a science project together last year?"

"Dad, the teacher assigned partners. Iggy would

never choose to spend time with Mike. Ever." She turned, belligerently, to head back up to her room.

She stopped, spun on her heel. "If you focus on Iggy, you'll never find that girl." It upset her to hear her father speak ill of the boy she once loved… maybe still did…

"You just leave the investigation to me," he insisted firmly before meeting her eyes with empathy. "I'll find her."

*

The worn out brass bell over the door of the pizza place rattled instead of rang when Iggy walked in. Greasy's name could have come from any number of things. The disgusting floor, the dirty walls, or the hair of its owner, Giuseppe. Officially, though, the name "Greasy" stemmed from the pizza that had been known to take up to four napkins to soak up the grease pool that formed in the center of the thin, cheesy pizza pies. Even a statement on the box warned not to set it on your car seat, or you'd have a permanent stain from the grease by the time you reached your home.

With a cigarette hanging from his lips and ashes falling carelessly into the dough, Giuseppe rolled a large, mushy circle on the counter. The dim lights were dulled further by the cloud of smoke haunting the ceiling. Iggy gagged a little when the cancer-laced cloud entered his lungs.

"Can I help a' you?" asked the grungy Italian with an extremely thick accent.

"Just waiting for someone," Iggy answered, coughing. "You know that secondhand smoke can kill people?"

Giuseppe pointed at the table by the front window. "Sit in the no smoking a' section."

Iggy rolled his eyes and walked over to the Pac Man machine. Arcade games lined one wall of the pizza shop, empty tables covered with crumbs and smudged fingerprints filled the others. He reached in his pocket for a quarter, noticed random green pine needles on the dirty wood floor.

"It's a' not working," Giuseppe's voice rang out from the open kitchen accompanied by a barking cough that crackled from his chest.

Iggy's shoulders sagged, and he moved to the pinball machine.

"It's a' broken... too," the store owner uttered. This time his words trailed off. Sliding to his left, Iggy started to put a quarter in the Super Mario game.

"That's a' no good either, my friend," Giuseppe called out once more.

Iggy pointed, frustrated, at the billiards table. "Does it work? Can I play pool?"

Giuseppe smiled and signaled an A-OK sign. "Works a' perfect!"

Finally! Iggy placed four quarters into the slots and shoved the lever forward, forcing the coins into the mechanism. The balls dropped down with a thud and rolled to the opening in the front of the table. Iggy grabbed them and placed them into the plastic, triangle rack, black 8 ball in the middle.

With the cue ball in hand, he moved to the other

end and placed it into position. Iggy rubbed the blue cube chalk on the end of one of the wooden sticks from the rack on the wall and lined up his first shot. Closing one eye, he focused on the abused, white ball. He moved the stick back and forth, gently, and then *SMACK!*

He thrusted the long stick ahead and sent the cue ball smashing into the group of balls at the other end. They scattered; one even fell into the corner pocket. When it did, the bell over the door chimed again.

"Igor," Mike said, like he was surprised to see him. "Playing against no one, so you can finally win at something?"

"I'm just waiting for someone."

"Let me guess... Liz Jackson? The love of your life?" Mike gave a phony look of condolence and then laughed. "That girl is over you, Igor. You blew it. In fact, I might ask her out myself."

Blood rushed to Iggy's face. He wanted to punch Mike, but took another shot at the pool table instead. Mike grabbed a stick, rubbed the end with chalk, and joined the game without permission from Iggy. He pointed to the side pocket and drilled the green, striped 14 ball directly into it.

"You spend any time with Jade over the summer, Mike?" pried Iggy, while Mike slammed another ball in. This time the corner pocket.

"You kidding?" Mike shrugged off the question. "That girl is a freak. I think she's demented."

"Oh, really?" Iggy coyly played along. "Yeah, you wouldn't spend any time with her, especially in the pines, right?"

Mike looked up from the table. Iggy had known him for years, but had never seen a look as frightening from him as the one Mike was giving right then. "What are you talking about?"

Iggy stood tall, trying his best to be intimidating. "The pines. At the school."

While slinging a gooey mass of cold pizza dough, Giuseppe's ears perked up in the kitchen when he heard Iggy mention the pines. He left a white coat of flour on his chin when he pulled the cigarette from his lips and flicked off the loose ashes with his thumb.

"I *know* what pines, Dummy. Why are you asking about Jade?" Mike asked, puffing his chest.

"Does it bother you?" Iggy meddled. His heart pounded, and Iggy tried to disguise his nervousness from his adversary.

Mike just sneered and returned to the pool table. One ball after another dropped in until he had the 8 ball lined up for an easy win.

The bell over the door dinged again, interrupting Mike's shot. Chief Jackson entered and stood accusingly over the boys at the pool table. Giuseppe watched, inconspicuously, bracing himself against the countertop with unsteady knees. Beads of sweat began to form on his face and arms. He inhaled a deep breath wearily. He blinked his eyes and shook his head gathering himself.

"Hi, Mr. Jackson," Iggy said uncomfortably.

"Iggy," the large man politely replied.

"Boom!" Mike exclaimed, sinking the final ball for the win. "You suck at this game, Igor." He raised up, placed his stick back on the rack, and glared at Jackson.

"Michael," said the chief. "Do you need to use

that kind of language?"

Mike slowly meandered up to Chief Jackson, closer than what would usually seem acceptable. "You know, Sir, I just can't think of another word that could better describe the way Igor plays this game other than *sucks.*"

Instead of taking the bait and returning Mike's aggression, Jackson retreated and put a little space between himself and the bold boy.

"Chief a' Jackson," called out Giuseppe after collecting himself, "I knew it wazza' you when a' you called before you even told me your a' name."

"I don't doubt it, Giuseppe." The chief kept his eyes on the two boys. "Don't you two wait too long to start home. You don't want to be caught out after dark. There is a curfew now."

"Yes Sir," Iggy said, obediently.

Mike, shaking his shoulders for a dramatic effect, forced a laugh from his belly. "Okay," he said, holding his hands up and overacting purposely. "Don't arrest me," he begged, sarcastically, and moved towards the door. He stopped short of it.

Iggy's heart began to thump in his chest. He realized that Mike had stopped to look at the poster of Sissy Daniels. Mike just stopped, like he'd quickly been turned to stone by the wicked stare of an evil witch. Chief Jackson and Giuseppe also took notice. Ten, twenty, thirty seconds passed, and Mike still stared at the image of the missing girl.

Chief Jackson and Iggy glanced at each other, and finally Mike whirled, dramatically, to face the others. He seemed distraught, breathing heavily. He just gawked at them, then grabbed the door, and yanked it open. The bell on the top jingled, and then Mike slammed the door, viciously, behind him.

"Iggy, go home. Elizabeth won't be able to meet you this afternoon," the Chief of Police informed. "If you're smart, you won't hang around that kid anymore."

Iggy nodded, silently.

"You tell your aunt and uncle that I said hello, please," Chief Jackson added.

"I will," Iggy said with a nod and then placed his

pool stick on the table and exited.

Giuseppe's eyes were large, red and watery, when he looked at the chief. "Those boys, they were talking about a' the pines."

"What did you hear?" Jackson whispered.

Giuseppe shook his head, his long, unwashed hair swayed from under his white hat, while he handed over the grease soaked pizza box in exchange for cash. "Not sure. But, I hear many a' things in a' here," he pointed to his hairy ear. "The kids all talk but a' they never realize how a' much I listen."

"You know anything about that girl on the poster?" Jackson motioned towards the picture with his head.

Giuseppe put his hand over his mouth, and his chest heaved up and down with his breaths. He nodded and squinted his eyes.

"What do you know, Giuseppe?" Jackson timidly asked for information, afraid of the answer he might hear.

"That girl," the frantic Italian said, pointing at the poster with his arm fully extended. "She..."

"She *what*?"

"She..." Tears welled in his lower eyelids and he blinked rapidly

"Giuseppe, she *what*?"

CRASH!

Giuseppe fell to the floor with a thud, like a bag of flour being dropped from two stories high.

"Giuseppe!" alarmingly shouted Chief Jackson. He jumped over the counter, kneeled next to the store owner, shook him, and then slapped his cheek to wake him.

"Giuseppe, are you okay?!"

The pizza shop owner, unresponsive and white as chalk, laid motionless on the grimy floor amongst dried bits of pepperoni and moldy pieces of mozzarella. Chief Jackson reached up and grabbed the phone from the wall and pressed 9-1-1.

"I need an ambulance right now! Greasy's! Hurry!"

*

One year ago…

He looked at the desperation in his wife's stare. Her pleads had evolved, over time, into profuse begging. His concern for her, the woman he loved, his beautiful, perfect partner, was outweighed by his fear. Fear of believing in something unexplainable, otherworldly even.

"Why can't you believe me?" she whispered into his ear, wrapping her arm over his chest, as they laid next to each other. He looked away, up at the ceiling. What was happening? Was his wife going crazy?

Her lip quivered as her heart sank. The man she trusted more than any other person on Earth couldn't even look her in the eye anymore. She sobbed into his shoulder, made a fist, and held his night shirt tightly.

Her claims were wild, her evidence questionable. "What would it take?" she would often ask herself. What would it take for him to just believe? He slid his arm under her back, feeling her shake as tears soaked her cheeks. He wiped them away, told her he loved her, and kissed her forehead. As she cried until sleep, he told himself she must be wrong, must be mistaking.

They *could not be real; they could not exist.*

Those things must just be in her mind, in her imagination.

They *had to be.*

Chapter 6

Tuesday – 4:37 pm

Listening, Mike paced on the sidewalk in front of his home. One would think a sound like that would just skip past a person's ears after hearing it for so long. It didn't. Instead of fading, it worsened over time. He hesitatingly kicked the ground, not wanting to go inside of his own house. Maybe he could slip in, unnoticed. The problem was, it seemed the only times he got noticed is when he wished he wouldn't be.

Just go straight to my room, thought Mike. That was the plan. He opened the front door, and the voices grew louder.

"I swear you don't appreciate anything I do around here!" his mother shrieked at his father. Her accusation filled with resentment.

"Maybe if you didn't burn everything you cooked, I *would* appreciate it!" his father roared back.

They were in the kitchen where they couldn't see their only son had entered the house. The boy stood in the living room where, visually, the place appeared peaceful. Nice furniture, some antiques, even a beautiful skyline painting of the city his mother grew up in hung on display over the expensive, large screen television. It was a facade, an illusion. It was the image of what his mother wished their home was really like. The awful screams from the kitchen told a much different story.

Just stay quiet, Mike told himself. He felt a sourness in his stomach when he heard shattering glass followed by more shouting and weeping. They would fight, his father would break something, his mother would wail. It was standard.

Mike just hoped that one day his father didn't break *her*. The police had been out several times, but, luckily, his father had never actually hurt her. Not bad enough for a hospital visit, anyway. Sometimes Mike wished that maybe he would. Then perhaps they would take his father away. Things could get better if his parents weren't at each other's throat day after day.

Maybe.

He closed his bedroom door after slipping past his arguing parents and pulled some photographs from an envelope that sat on his desk. He laid them all out, side by side. They were pictures taken of the pines behind the school. They were unclear, captured close to dusk. Looking at each one over and over, relentlessly, he studied them.

He pulled out another envelope with more photos inside. One was a picture of Principal Warren walking on the baseball diamond between the pines and the school. Another was of Giuseppe, leaving Greasy's late one night.

The seventh-grader had become an instant pro at using the one-hour-photo service at the pharmacy. Mike would drop off his roll of film at the counter and they would have them ready for pickup sixty minutes later.

Mike's room was filled with trophies, blue ribbons, first place plaques. A natural at everything he had ever attempted, save school work, that is. Sports were easy for him. He was the best at all of them. However, as great as he was, he couldn't recall even one single time his parents had come to watch him play. Maybe once when he was in T-ball, but definitely not since then.

Hearing a thump in the hallway, he shook. The argument had worked its way from the kitchen towards his bedroom. Even louder now, his father cursed and then the front door slammed rattling all the windows. And then silence. Mike breathed relief briefly until his bedroom door swung open.

"Mikey," his mother whimpered, face wet with tears. "How was your day, honey?"

Mike didn't want to look at her. "Fine, Mom."

"Your dad's drunk again. Came home that way," she muttered, taking a swig from a beer bottle.

"Can you shut the door, Mom? I have homework."

"You're just like him!" she screeched. "You're gonna be just like him!"

"Mom! Shut the door!"

She slammed it. Her voice faded down the hall,

inaudible.

He didn't cry about it anymore, not like he used to. Night after night, year after year, he would fall asleep sobbing into his pillow, scared of what might happen. Never knowing if one morning he'd wake to find one, or both, of them dead.

*

Music blared through the headphones into Jade's ears. The cryptic melody of The Cure's "Lovesong" soaked through her entire being. Cross legged on her bed, she drew in her sketch book. Her memory was strong, able to remember fine details of images she'd seen. Her drawings proved it.

The lonely girl's face on the page was the spitting image of Sissy Daniels. Behind the missing girl were pines, tall and dark, towering over top of her.

Between the trees, popping through the shadowy layers of pencil lead, were eyes. Some large, some small, these eyes peered at Sissy. Jade carefully retraced each edge, defining them with the silver pencil lead.

After a while, she walked out to the living room where her father and stepmother were combatting in a game of chess. They considered the pieces on the board, intently, until they noticed her enter the room. An orange and yellow fire flickered in the brick fireplace behind them making their shadows dance on the wallpaper.

"Hello, Sweetie," her father said with a gentle, warm smile.

"Hey, Dad."

"Homework all done?" he wondered, averting his eyes back to the board.

"Yeah, just wanna get a snack," she assured him.

Her stepmom stood up, "Let me get you something, Dear," she offered.

"It's okay. You guys are playing. I can get it."

"I insist. I can make you a grilled cheese." Jade's stepmom made the world's best grilled cheese sandwiches, the perfect amount of garlic and pepper and the bread burned exactly to Jade's liking. The cheese notoriously stretched between the two halves when pulled apart.

Jade smiled, with hungry appreciation.

"I think the new season of Full House starts tonight," the substitute mother shared.

"Cool," Jade responded. Her life was pretty good, usually uneventful, and safe. Her dad was well off financially and, honestly, her stepmom was a wonderful addition to the family. Jade, as badly as she wanted to, didn't have much to gripe about. She was given most anything she wanted, whenever she wanted it. TV in her room, computer, whatever music albums she desired.

Her parents weren't invasive or nosy. She'd earned their trust over the years and that was valuable, like money in the bank. It was something she didn't want to lose. So, regardless of the image she had at school, mysterious and aloof, at home she was just Daddy's little girl. Innocent and respectful. She, a great student and a hard worker, would never admit or demonstrate publicly those qualities to the other kids in her class. The students all knew her as an enigmatic loner, a rebel with little regard for authority.

And that's the way Jade liked it.

*

Pushing the food around on his plate, Iggy sulked at the dinner table. He hated vegetables; his aunt loved to prepare them. She cooked every night for her nephew and her husband, Uncle Joe. Been that way since the accident. Iggy had been under Aunt Beth's and Uncle Joe's care for just about three years. The parentless boy moved into their home the week it all transpired. Although the memories were slowly diminishing, Iggy still was able to conjure up the way he felt back then. Revisiting those feelings was never fun.

He finished enough of his meal to reasonably justify excusing himself from the table. Small talk over dessert in front of the television would satisfy his aunt and uncle for the night. *How was school? Do you have any homework?* Questions adults had to ask, but rarely cared to hear the full details.

Retiring to his room, he grabbed the phone off the

hook and dialed Liz's number. Uncle Joe had gotten him a private line for his birthday last year, since Iggy and Liz spent almost every waking second on the phone together. But it hadn't gotten much use lately.

Home alone, Liz seized the cordless phone off her bed. "Hello?"

Instead of posters of actors and singers, her walls were covered with beautiful pictures of endangered species. Tigers, pandas, even a picture of Earth with *Save the Planet* printed on it hung boldly by the mirror. Stuffed animals, piled high on her bed and bookcase, always kept her company. Not Care Bears and Disney Characters, but ones that looked real. Detailed accurately, beautifully. Her mother had been an animal activist. A warrior for the environment before she fell suddenly ill, a couple years after the accident that took Iggy's parents away.

About one year ago, actually. Liz's mom lost her battle to the sickness, but Liz kept her memory alive and well.

"Hey, it's me," Iggy said, happy to hear Liz's voice.

"Hey," she greeted him, equally glad to hear his, yet less eager to show it.

"I saw your dad at Greasy's."

"He told me. He's at the hospital with Giuseppe. Giuseppe passed out, and I guess he still hasn't woken up."

"Whoa. Really?" Iggy exclaimed, surprised. He was just with Giuseppe.

"Yeah, Dad said you were with Mike. Did you get any information out of him?" she wondered.

"No, he just had a strange reaction when he saw Sissy's picture on the wall. Same reaction he had in the gym. Creepy," Iggy paused. "He told me he would never, ever hang out with Jade."

"And Jade said the same about Mike, too," Liz reported, racking her brain for times when she might have seen the two of them together at some point over the years. She couldn't find one.

"Something isn't right. The necklace, the note, secret meetings. What do you think they are meeting in the morning for?"

"I don't know, but I know what I'll be doing," Iggy told her, prompting her to ask about his intentions.

"What?"

He smiled, convinced she wouldn't be able to resist joining him once he notified her of his plans. "Going to the pines before the police start looking again."

"What about the after sunset curfew?"

"Technically, at that time in the morning, it will have stopped being *after sunset* and started being *before sunrise*."

"They're looking for the girl there. If we can link Mike and Jade to the pines..."

Iggy finished her thought, "Then maybe we can prove they're hiding what happened to her."

Chapter 7

Wednesday – 5:40 am

Mike stood in the backyard, under his bedroom window. It was still dark, pitch black. The yard light made the fog appear even denser than it already was. He waited, eagerly. He looked at the house, wondering if his parents were up, what they would do if they knew he was outside about to leave. Would it be cause for screaming? Maybe a beating? It was worth the risk.

He'd be in trouble for something before the end of the day anyway, and things had gotten out of hand. If he waited too much longer to act, it might be too late. He watched closely as the bushes that lined the yard began to stir.

Mike heard a twig snap and knew it was finally time. His heart thumped as Jade's pale face glowed under the lamp through the mist.

"Hey," she said, approaching him.

"Hey," he replied, handing her a beat-up notebook.

She opened it to the first page and began to read the list in her head. Her eyes darted up at Mike. "Jackson? You sure?"

He shook his head. "No, I'm not sure about him. But the rest I'm certain about."

"Lizard will be... devastated," she worried, softly.

"Yes, I know. And it would complicate things even further."

"This is getting scary," Jade said, scanning the dark trees and shadows for unwanted guests behind Mike with her eyes.

"If Jackson is involved, and they end up finding Sissy, he's going to come after me. I won't stand a chance," Mike said with concern.

She touched his arm, smoothly. "It's not too late. We have some time before school. We should get moving. Every second counts."

Mike agreed, and they both walked from the yard light into the darkness of Lakewood.

*

Iggy and Liz met up in *their* spot by the swings and began to walk, side by side. Dressed for school, they weaved in and out of yards and driveways walking the way-the-crow-flies to the middle school. No need to abide by the streets and sidewalks at that time of day.

"What are we looking for?" she asked him.

He wanted to hold her hand but didn't. "Anything. Those pines are connected to this girl's disappearance. Connected to Mike and Jade, too. We have to see what's out there."

He looked at her captivating, brown eyes. One kiss would change everything. Would he get a chance to try? One kiss would bring her heart back to him. He was sure of it.

"It's quiet," she observed about the town. "Feels normal right now. The way it was when I left."

"Yeah," he agreed, watching the toe of his sneaker kick a pebble. "When the sun comes up, though, nothing is the same anymore. Missing kids, cops in school, Italians passing out in the pizza shop." She smiled at him. She had always found Iggy's sense of humor intriguing.

He knew it, too and winked at her. "I heard Dave Jensen called you."

She stopped. Iggy followed suit. "He did," she admitted.

"Are you going to go out with him?"

She raised her eyebrows. "Seriously?" Her eyes were gorgeous. Iggy could hardly stand to look into them without pleading with her to reconsider their breakup.

"It's just that... I mean, I just know he called you," he sputtered out, suddenly feeling foolish.

"My dad would *never* let me date a high-schooler. Besides, I wouldn't want to anyway." She started walking again.

"I just..."

"You know me better than that, Iggy."

Without speaking, they continued. Iggy's heart was soft, thinking that maybe she still had feelings for him. It was strange, because for the first time he could remember, he was unable to read her, powerless to figure out what was going on inside of her.

Their shoulders bumped, as they moved downhill towards the school yard. The smell of her perfume entered Iggy's nostrils, sending his mind elsewhere. She had always worn that kind, the kind her mother wore. In fact, her mom used to make the perfume in their garage, like some sort of mad scientist, and even though neighbors teased her for it, she never cared.

So many of Iggy's memories of Liz were triggered by the scent of the strong, yet delicate fragrance. And every single memory that he had mattered now. Birthday parties, church Christmas programs, random school lunch periods. No matter how unimportant some moments were, they stuck in his mind, and he fought to hold them there, to keep them vivid.

Even the most meaningless event with Liz was now significant, knowing he may not have any more of them with her by his side. They had been the school's power couple, but they were even more than that. Their affection was real. He had always loved Liz and always would. Before the end of school last spring he had never doubted they'd always be together. But, now he wondered...

She used to be taller than him, but now they were the same height. He had caught up and was sure to go past her, like boys often did at their age. Iggy knew they were meant to be. He *knew* it. She used to know it, too. But now he'd have to convince her of it. With all that was happening in Lakewood, the thought of going through life without Liz is what scared him the most.

"There it is," she pointed out, breaking the silence.

"The Pines," he stated with an eerie, haunting sound to his voice. She smiled at him again.

"You ready for this?" she asked him, raising her eyebrows with uncertainty.

He nodded and raised the yellow police tape for her to crouch under. They slid into the dark edge of the pines. The trees, tall and daunting, seemed to disappear into the black morning sky. Fog mingled with the pines, coursing in and out, between the sticky, sap covered branches. Pinecones and a thick layer of brown needles covered the ground.

Crunching under every step, Liz and Iggy looked at each other, asking *"Was that you?"* with their eyes each time they heard the slightest noise. She stayed close to him, bumped him occasionally, and finally gripped his jacket. She trusted him.

Liz's secure grasp comforted Iggy. She still looked to him for *something*, at least. Visibility was low, but they kept trudging through. Every step required more effort than the last, as the prickly, needle covered branches seemed to reach out and attempt to stop them. Their pace slow, but steady - determined. The pines appeared endless.

Crunch... crunch... crunch.

Their heads both jerked to the front right, then their eyes locked. Iggy nodded, confirming to Liz that he also heard what she did.

Crunch... crunch... crunch.

They halted. Iggy felt Liz's cold fingers entwine with his.

"It's probably a deer," he said into her ear, her curly hair tickled his nose, her cheek close to his lips, her perfume intoxicating him.

She observed Iggy, eyes wide, and huffed an anxious breath. She let go of his hand, to his dismay. "Okay, let's keep going then," she suggested.

They went deeper, now feeling silly for being so scared earlier. Iggy inhaled and could smell Liz's perfume again. "What's your dad going to think when he wakes up and you're gone?" he asked.

"I left a note that I had to be at school early," she whispered back. "He was out late working on the case. Probably won't be up too early anyway."

Iggy grinned. She had always been tough. You would assume that being the Chief of Police's daughter would be enough to keep her away from trouble. And in a way, it had. Liz rarely was in any trouble--because she was so good at avoiding being caught. Being the chief's daughter meant having to be able to sneak out under the keenest eye. She was a master.

They entered a small clearing, a tiny opening in the thickly growing pine trees.

There, right before them, it stood thin, feeble, and small. A pine tree no taller than they were.

Iggy's flashlight shined on it. It looked vibrant next to the older, weather-worn trees that surrounded it. The other pines were four, five, six times its height. Liz reached her hand out, let one of its needles prick her fingertip. Silently, they stared.

Crunch… crunch… crunch.

Their heads spun, looking for what made that sound.

"Those are footsteps," she whispered as she nervously pivoted her head watching several directions at once.

Crunch… crunch… crunch… crunch.

Iggy spied to the left, then the right. "What direction are they coming from?" he asked in hushed tones.

"The right," she insisted.

Crunch... crunch.

"I mean left."

Crunch... crunch.

"It's coming from behind us," Iggy warned.

Crunch... crunch.

"I mean in front of us." He pulled his flashlight out, pointed it ahead. The beam of light blew back in his face, reflecting off the fog and not helping to see even slightly.

"There!" Liz pointed. A lone figure moved, as a shadow, from tree to tree.

"Here, too!" Iggy exclaimed, quietly. Another moved to his right.

The sound of footsteps was all around, circling Iggy and Liz, surrounding them. They turned, back to back, feeling trapped, uncertain which way to run. Reaching down, their hands locked instinctively. This time she didn't let go, but squeezed tightly instead.

The soft murmur of voices crept under the sound of the breaking pine needles. Moans, not words, filled their ears.

"Iggy," she choked, turning her lean body towards his and buried her face into his shoulder.

His eyes scanned in all directions, the sounds closed in on them. Her hand in his, he pulled her, running.

The sun climbed out from behind the night, bringing the shadows to life. Iggy could distinguish several of them, but only silhouettes, the shaded etchings of human form.

Iggy and Liz then erupted into a full speed run. Pine needles flew off the branches as they crashed through the thick forest. Twigs and pinecones crunched and scattered under their feet. Like arms, the tree branches grabbed at them, slapped against their bodies, but they sprinted, blindly onward. Finally, leaving the noises behind, they busted out of the pines and slipped under the police tape.

Breathing heavily, they faced at each other shaking with panicked, wide eyes.

"Were those... police... officers? Looking for that... girl?" Iggy panted, fighting to catch his breath.

She shook her head. "No, Iggy... I don't think so."

"Look!" he yelled, pointing.

Out of the repressive pines surged Mike. He raced, full tilt, across the baseball diamonds. He never looked back, never stopped until he reached the rear entrance of the school and blew through the door, out of sight.

Chapter 8

Wednesday – 8:15 am

"Iggy?" called Mr. Miller. Three days in, and he already stopped including last names while taking attendance.

"Here," Iggy confirmed; he had made it to his desk on time. He picked a pine needle out of his sock, flicked it to the floor.

Bing.

"Good morning, students," Principal Warren's voice blasted through the intercom that hung over the clock at the front of the room. "Let's have another great day at Lakewood Pines Middle School."

Mr. Miller looked up at the intercom speaker, gleaming. "We have a great principal," he announced before continuing roll call.

All the kids responded, "*Here*" while they sorted through their homework, double checking it one last time.

"Elizabeth?"

"Here," she answered, trying to rub pine sap off the knee of her faded jeans.

"Mike?" the teacher then called out. Hearing nothing, he looked up from his attendance log. "Mr. Lawman?" he blurted, staring at Mike.

"What?" Mike asked, gruffly.

"I'm taking attendance," Mr. Miller informed. Slouching in his chair, Mike looked at him. "Well, are you here?" the educator sarcastically asked.

Mike lowered his eyes to his own twiddling thumbs. "Are you blind, Mr. Miller?"

Mr. Miller's face reddened angrily. "I don't appreciate that remark, Mr. Lawman."

"I wasn't trying to flatter you," Mike replied, still gazing down as he traced a sappy smudge line on the back of his hand.

"Watch your tone," the teacher ordered him with angst.

Mike's head popped up. "Why don't you send me down to Principal Warren's office?"

Mr. Miller stared at Mike, almost as a contest, first one to look away loses. "I wouldn't waste Principal Warren's time on you, Mike. You're not *worth* his time."

Mike gripped the front of his desk with both hands and pulled himself up from his lazy position. With his seat in the front row, he sat only a few feet from Mr. Miller. Mike squinted. "I'm *HERE!!!*" he yelled with a growling tone at the top of his lungs.

Their stare down continued, while Mike slowly returned to his slouch. Mr. Miller went back to his list of names, not acknowledging Mike's audacious challenge of his authority.

Liz glimpsed at Iggy and shrugged. The kids in class exchanged looks, confused. All their older siblings and cousins had been telling them that Mr. Miller was no pushover. He had a reputation for being nice, but tough on troublemakers.

"He takes no crap," Iggy's next door neighbor told him over the summer. Mike, by all accounts, should have been on his way to Principal Warren's office, but instead he still sat in his seat, having seemingly forced Mr.

Miller to surrender. *What gives?*

"Jade," the teacher called. "Jade?" He looked up then back down, making a check mark in his book.

Liz turned to investigate. Jade wasn't there. Her eyes grew large, Iggy's did too. Where *was* she? They knew for a fact that she was meeting Mike that morning.

Had she been in the pines with him too?

What could've happened to her?

*

Beeps from the monitor connected to Giuseppe hummed steadily, rhythmically. Tired, Chief Jackson wiped his palm down his face, urging himself to wake up.

"Any idea what happened to him?" he asked, as the short haired nurse entered with a stethoscope around her neck.

"The doctor isn't certain," she testified with her hands on her hips. "Is he in some sort of trouble or something?"

At first, Jackson didn't understand, but then

realized she was asking him because he was wearing his police uniform. "Oh, no. No trouble. Just want to ask him about something."

"The missing girl?" she guessed, while checking all of Giuseppe's vital signs.

"Yeah, how did you know?"

"Well, Giuseppe lives across the street from the pines. I saw your search team yesterday." She adjusted the IV unit, slowing the rate at which the medicine was administered. "Can you believe how cold it's been for September? The leaves have almost all fallen already."

Chief Jackson watched Giuseppe and wondered what he knew about the pines and Sissy. "Sure has been cold," he said, without looking at the attentive woman. "If I leave my number here by the phone, can you give me a call if his condition changes?"

"Of course," she granted. "You're the Chief of Police, after all."

He smiled. "Thank you, ma'am." He tipped his cap towards her, "You have a nice day now."

She smiled back. Jackson, handsome and polite,

always could get a return smile from everyone, especially love starved nurses who spent their evenings reading supermarket romance novels.

He jotted his phone number at the police station along with his home number on a pad by the room telephone. The nurse left him with a flirtatious grin that he deflected with grace.

He crouched over the white sheets, studying Giuseppe's expressionless face. The Italian's breathing was slow, his appearance peaceful.

"What information do you have for me, Pizza Man?" Jackson whispered. He turned around, confirming the nurse was gone and quickly grabbed Giuseppe's chart from the wall. He read it and flipped to the second page, then back to the first.

"It can't be," he told himself. He looked at the unconscious patient again.

"I can't believe it." He put the clipboard back on the wall and exhaled deeply. He shook off his worried face, exited the room, and left Giuseppe alone with the steady beeps that followed his heartbeat.

*

Crash!

Trying to rid the stinging in her elbow that came from breaking the window, she rubbed her arm. She looked around and checked for witnesses before plucking the remaining shards of glass from the wooden pane. She hopped through the window frame and loosened the drawstring that held her black hood tightly around her apprehensive face. Breaking and entering wasn't her thing, but with the evidence piled so high, she was left with no choice. It had to be done.

Her breathing jumped nervously, her heart fluttered uneasily, as she explored the dark room. She knew the place was empty but still flinched at every sound, afraid someone would be in the next room waiting for her.

She banged her shin on the coffee table, uttered a word her parents wouldn't have approved of, and pressed her hand on the numb spot.

That'll bruise, for sure.

"Slow down," she coached herself. "You shouldn't have come if you were going to screw it up."

Pausing a moment to calm herself, she clenched her fists by her side and ventured on, determined to get this right. She stopped and grumbled when she entered the kitchen, then spun on her heel, quickly exiting.

Not the kitchen, stupid! It wouldn't be in there.

She stubbed her foot on the nightstand in the bedroom, nearly tipping the lamp over. She steadied it and checked over her shoulder for someone. No one was there, of course.

Rummaging through his things seemed shady to her, criminal even. Technically, it probably was. She warded off any second guessing. Too late for that. Too much at stake. Bedroom was clean.

Back into the living room, she could see the pines through the window. What secrets had been viewed through it? From that room? She turned down the back hall and opened a door near the end of it.

What she expected to be a linen closet was

actually more than that. It was an office. The person that lived here obviously hadn't anticipated having an intruder. That was clear by the way he stored his keys-- hanging on a tack board, clearly labeled.

Garage.
Shed.
Front entrance.
Car spare.
Alley door.

Got it.

*

"This rain is killing us!" bellowed Mr. Armstrong. He blew his shrill whistle. "Line up!"

The boys ran to their assigned places on the gym floor. All of them spaced out in rows, like a grid. "Jumping Jacks!" he barked and he whistled once more.

The entire class jumped and raised their arms with Mr. Armstrong counting them off, like a drill sergeant in the army.

"Halt!" he shouted after reaching the number twenty.

The lesser fit kids were already huffing and wheezing from exercise. Iggy kept an eye on Mike, looking for any odd behavior, which was not easy. Mike's behavior was always odd.

"Down on the floor! Pushups!" The whistle resonated again. The boys all dropped to their stomachs, and Mr. Armstrong began counting, as they all moved their bodies up and down with their arms.

*

"I just wish I could fill my bathtub with yogurt," Ms. Cain announced to no one. "Oh, how wonderful the cold, silky cream would feel all over me, between my toes, in my armpits. I would do strawberry, I think. No, peach."

Liz sat, staring at the empty desk beside her. She

turned to look at the poster with Sissy Daniels' smiling face, and wondered if one with Jade's image would show up next. Principal Warren's stride broke her gaze, as he entered the room. His walk was confident, bold; his voice the same.

"Good morning, Students." He dawdled over to Ms. Cain's desk and revealed a cup of nonfat, peach yogurt from behind his back. She was thrilled.

"Thank you, Principal Warren," she exalted with her hand on her heart. "You've read my mind. I was just talking about slipping into a bath of peach yogurt." She swallowed her emotions, holding back a tear of joy. Special attention from the handsome principal always made her feel warm inside.

"Now that would sure be a sight to see," he uttered with a wink.

Her eyes glazed over with gushing appreciation. "Thank you," she whispered so low it was nearly inaudible.

"You're very welcome," he assured her, turning to the class. "Kids, you may have noticed the search team at the pines yesterday."

No one spoke. Everyone paid close attention.

"I've been asked to let all the students know that anyone that goes into the pines could hurt the ongoing investigation into the disappearance of Sissy Daniels." He paused awkwardly when his eye landed on the desk where Jade should have been sitting.

He realized that the kids were all waiting for him to continue and quickly poised himself. "Please, stay out of the pines until further notice."

He touched Liz's desk with his long, scrawny fingers. "Hello, Elizabeth," he said, straining. He twitched his nose, pressed his temple with his fist, and made a small grunting sound. He opened his mouth, flexed his jaw, like he was working a rusty hinge.

She nodded to him, "Good morning, Sir."

He turned back to Ms. Cain who was intently staring at her boss. "Sorry, to interrupt," he apologized.

Smitten by his gift, she batted her eyes at him as he left. She slurped peach yogurt off her spoon, making a gurgling sound.

"A bath of peach yogurt," she imagined. "I'd do it, but I'm afraid I'd eat it all." No one was listening, as she laughed, amused by her own words.

Liz glanced over at Jade's empty desk again and knew that Principal Warren had also been alarmed. Maybe Jade was sick or at a doctor's appointment?

Maybe?

*

On the floor, legs spread like Vs, the boys all had their heads down, as they stretched their muscles out. They peeked up as they heard the sound of high priced, leather dress shoes clicking on the hardwood floor. When Mr. Armstrong finished his ten count, they looked up and saw Principal Warren whispering into the gym teacher's ear.

Iggy watched as Mr. Armstrong slapped his own shoulder, like a mosquito was biting it. He rubbed it, firmly, before easing the pressure. The coach whispered something back; Principal Warren pressed his index finger against his temple, then quickly looked at Mike

Lawman.

"Stand up, Lawman," yelled Mr. Armstrong.

Mike didn't respond immediately but eventually obeyed the command. With the rest of the class still seated, Mike stood, solitary. The principal marched to him, covering a large distance, while the kids all watched.

"I need you in my office, Mr. Lawman!" he barked, standing only feet from Mike. Half of the class jumped from surprise. Mike put his head down and walked out of the gym. Principal Warren followed close behind him.

*

One year ago...

Staring down at the small pile of pine needles on her desk, she began to doubt herself and her hypothesis. She grabbed the glass, ball shaped bottle with a spray top and squeezed it in her sweaty palm. She closed her eyes, wished, hoped. She plucked one green needle from the stack, isolated it on the table a few inches from the others.

"Here goes," she said to herself and sprayed the contents of the bottle on the single needle. The mist floated down, in slow motion, as she waited for it to make contact. Softly, it fell, touching the green, stick-like, piece of evergreen. Steam, smoke, something mist-like began to rise from it. She gasped. The pine needle twitched, almost appeared to come to life, then shriveled and burned into ashes.

She took another, laid it down, and sprayed it. Again, she saw the same effect: steam, twitch, shrivel.

Excitement flooded her insides. She squirted the bottle, dousing the pile of pine needles with the potion. They burned into nothing, right before her eyes.

It worked! Whatever those things were that lived in the pines, walked the streets of Lakewood, the halls of the middle school, had finally met their match. More time was needed though, more preparation, more research. She would need more ingredients to make more of this magical liquid, this life saving mixture.

And maybe, just maybe, seeing this would finally

convince her husband of the evil that she and the pizza shop owner had uncovered.

Chapter 9

Wednesday – 3:33 pm

Shortly after Iggy's knuckles racked the bright red door of the Jackson house, Liz opened it. Their eyes did the talking as he entered. The smell of the cool air and misty rain followed through the doorway, attached to him. Her living room was cozy, as always, Iggy felt warm being there again. It had been a while. Evidently, the home missed Liz's mother. The room, unkempt, needed a dusting. The small touches and attention to detail the chief's wife had a knack for was a skill Jackson himself lacked.

Liz clicked off the television and silently sat next to him. So much had happened, many questions hovered over them, a lot had changed. In that moment, however, was the vague appearance of normalcy, a return to how it used to be. Iggy at Liz's after school, hanging out had been a staple of life for ages. Comfortable, commonplace, like home. As a captured image from the outside, it was the same as always.

But in reality, today was drastically different. She averted her eyes, feeling his on her, wanting to look at him, but refusing to. She looked at her fingernails then their reflection in the convex, black TV screen – at anything but him.

Their hearts were beating, nervously, in unison, waiting for the other to fill the quiet air between them.

"Where's your dad?" Iggy finally inquired, nearly choking on his words.

Her eyes darted to him, for a moment then retreated. "Working. Looking for the girl," she figured. "Or clues about her, I guess."

"It was Mike," Iggy blurted out.

"You think he killed her?"

Iggy hesitated, "I mean Mike started those rumors. The ones about you… About *us*."

She looked at him, wanting it to be true, wishing

it were. "Iggy, I don't want to talk about this."

"Okay," he quickly respected her stance, not wanting to upset her again.

Squashing the awkwardness before it could blossom, she turned back to the missing girl. "I think Mike did something to that girl," she said.

Iggy shrugged his shoulders. "He had the necklace. Or *some* necklace."

"He was in the pines this morning," she sat up straighter, slid a little closer.

"But, there were others, too."

"Jade?"

"Maybe. But, who else?"

"And how many?"

Iggy inched closer to her. "It was dark, confusing."

"You sure it wasn't just the two of them? Maybe it only seemed like more."

"Maybe..." he leaned back into the soft pillow sofa, exhaled, shook his head. "I don't buy it, Liz. I don't like Mike at all. But is he a killer?"

"Sometimes he has this look," she squinted, trying to copy it. "A gleam in his eye," she shivered, her skin crawled.

Iggy smiled. She was cute. "I know, I've seen it. I've been competing with Mike since we were six years old. It's always a contest, and, yes, he has a killer instinct on the court and on the field, but I just can't see him doing something like this." Iggy searched his memory of Mike. "No, I can't imagine him really hurting someone."

"What about hiding it? Concealing something?" Liz asked, looking deep into Iggy's eyes.

He wanted to kiss her. Resisting, he nodded. "Yes. That he could do. For sure. I agree that he knows something about what happened. Maybe was even there."

"I think he knows *exactly* what happened," Liz concluded. She grabbed a *MISSING* poster from the stack on the coffee table left there by her father.

She fell back on the pillow sofa, next to Iggy, and held it in front of them. Their shoulders, elbows rested together. She tipped her head, resting it on his shoulder.

"Look at her," she whispered. "She looks so

happy. So alive. She would've been in our grade."

Iggy nodded, moving as little as possible, hoping she didn't pick her head up. Her hair tickled his ear, but he held still. "Do you think she's actually dead?"

Liz sighed, "I wonder. I wonder that all the time. And I wonder what's going on around here. Things feel so..." A tear spilled over her bottom eyelid, streamed down her brown cheek. The salty liquid slipped between her lips.

"You don't have to worry. You're safe. Nothing's going to happen to you," Iggy consoled.

"I'm not worried about me. I'm worried about Sissy," she corrected him. He wasn't surprised, she'd always been fearless in his eyes.

"What if she is really dead, Iggy? What if someone murdered her? Someone from Lakewood. Or what if she's not dead and something terrible is happening to her *right now*?"

"I'll press Mike tomorrow," he promised. "I'll find out if he really does know something."

The front door popped open, and Chief Jackson's

shadow fell on the tiled foyer floor along with frantic drops of rain. Iggy and Liz raised up from the couch cushions, alert with *not guilty* pleas on their faces. She wiped the sticky trail left by her falling tear with her palm.

"Elizabeth, what is Iggy doing here?" he asked even with the rain still hitting his back.

Chief Jackson closed the door and sat his bag down next to the axe that always sat by the front door. *Happy Birthday, Sweetheart* was engraved beautifully on the wooden handle. Liz's mother bought it for her dad's birthday two years ago. It never made sense. It was a strange gift. A lot of what her mom did in the final years of her life hadn't made sense to the chief. But, he loved her until the end.

"Dad, we're just talking," Liz said, "about all that's been going on around here." Her father's critical eyes noticed the *MISSING* poster in her hand.

"Iggy, I don't expect you to be here when I'm not home," the chief said, sternly.

This was a new rule. Iggy cleared his throat, "Sir, I –,"

"Where were you last night, Iggy?"

Unsure why he was being asked this, the boy stuttered his reply, "I was h-h-home."

"All night? How about early this morning?"

"Dad, why are you - ," Liz started, quickly cut off.

"Jade Wilson hasn't been seen since she went to bed last night," Chief Jackson told them. "She's missing."

Any hope that Jade was home sick today vanished.

"Iggy, I want you to go home, straight home, stay there until it's time for school tomorrow. Understood?" The chief stomped his feet on the mat, knocking loose the pine needles clinging to his wet rubber boots.

Iggy stood up, but Liz grabbed his arm, pulling him back. "No! Dad, don't make him leave!"

Looking at her, Iggy could see it in her eyes: *love*. She still loved him. "It's okay," Iggy told her. "I'll see you at school tomorrow."

Straight-faced and defiant, he looked at Chief Jackson but obeyed him. Liz, fuming, ran up the stairs to her room. Iggy slid past the chief, brushing against him in order to pass by, and closed the door behind himself.

The phone blared a loud, synthetic ring. The chief lumbered over, knowing he was tracking on the carpet. He grimaced, mentally assigning himself the duty of cleaning up the mess later.

"Hello?" he said into the phone. "What? He's awake?"

He covered the mouthpiece with his hand, "Liz! Come down here. We're leaving!"

Lowering his voice, he removed his palm from covering the device, "I'll be right there."

*

"Stay here, Sweetie," Chief Jackson instructed his daughter. She sat on the vinyl gray seat outside of Giuseppe's hospital room. The fabric had cracks, torn from years of use by concerned friends and family members awaiting news about their ill loved ones. Their uncertainty had left a residue, an aura, blanketing the halls. Liz quietly watched a large, middle-aged nurse chase her father into the room.

Jackson viewed the unconscious Italian fidget, squirm on the bed. "He's awake?"

"No," the nurse said, "but he's been talking."

"What did he say?" the chief urgently asked, cringing uncomfortably at the man's involuntary movements.

"Mumbling mostly," she recalled, "Possibly in Italian, I guess."

"What's all this? What's this mess?" he pointed to the floor around the hospital bed.

"Pine needles," she answered.

"I can see that. Why are they here?"

She looked at Jackson, unsure. "We don't know."

They both flinch when Giuseppe let out a moan, a *noise*.

"Anyone around here speak Italian? This guy have any family?" Chief Jackson asked, feeling frightened. The creaking bed became louder, more aggressive.

She shook her head, "We couldn't even find a

next of kin to notify of his illness. We haven't seen any visitors. No one."

Another nurse with brown, shoulder-length hair that swayed as she walked and a tall, lanky female doctor rushed by Liz. As they opened Giuseppe's door, Liz looked over her shoulder but couldn't see in, just heard the commotion.

"Owe," she said, quickly pulling her hand off the chair. Looking at her palm, she could see a small indentation in her skin. A poke mark.

On Liz's chair was a pine needle. A long, green pine needle. She picked it up, held it in front of her, studying it. It was thick, coarse, strong. She put each end of it between her fingers, rolled it, feeling its edges.

She bent each end down, bowing the center. The ends got closer together. Closer until *snap*. She watched the needle break, then her eyes focused ahead, down the long hospital hallway.

A blurry figure faced her, staring from the far end of the corridor. When her eyes adjusted, she could see him. Mike Lawman.

For a second her eyes connected with his, but the elevator door behind him slid open and he slipped inside.

She sat up as the door sealed shut. Without thinking, she was up off her seat chasing. Liz sprinted, full stride down the hall, passing nurses pushing patients on beds saddled with IV units. She slammed her hand against the *down* button, but it was too late.

The elevator descended with Mike inside of it. The Lakewood Hospital was tiny, two stories high. She spun to her left, burst through the door leading to the stairway. She could beat the elevator down to the first floor, if she was fast enough!

Using the metal rail, she lifted herself, pivoting on her straight arms, spanning several steps at a time. She hit the midpoint landing, and did the same down the second set of stairs that faced in the opposite direction, finishing at the door that exited the staircase.

Liz yanked open the heavy metal barrier and stormed the lobby. On one side she saw the open elevator door, on the other she saw Mike running through the main entrance, out to the sidewalk. He was gone.

She shuffled her feet, disappointed, into the elevator and pressed the number 2. The door closed and she could smell it before she even saw them. It smelled like Christmas trees.

At her feet, all over the floor, dozens of long, green pine needles spotted the crisp white linoleum.

*

Chief Jackson's body quivered from the shrill sound of Giuseppe's scream. The horrific scene had worsened. The doctor and several nurses surrounded the pizza man's bed, shouting orders, reporting information. They all froze when it happened.

Goose pimples, large, like boils began to form on his face and neck. His convulsions intensified, even lifting his torso entirely off the bed, then sending it slamming back down, violently. The bumps swelled, turned red, then shrank and grew again, covering his entire body. They puffed, up and down; his body shook profoundly.

The hospital staff and Chief Jackson could only

observe, as he raised his head and screamed in horrific pain. "Pines!" The single syllable lasted several seconds, before his body went limp.

The room was suddenly quiet, save the monitor that followed the patient's heartbeat. Only it had changed. Now a long, high pitched, steady noise filled the air. The sound of an alarm clock with no pulse. The boils slowly disappeared into his pastel skin without a trace.

The staff was still, quiet, eyes filled with tears, as the doctor pronounced him *dead*.

Liz stood motionless in the hallway; Giuseppe's piercing last word resonated in her head. She watched her father, visibly shaken, exit Giuseppe's room.

Trailing behind him, Liz said nothing, as they left the hospital, headed for home.

Chapter 10

Wednesday – 7:47 pm

Mike's sneakers pounded the concrete hard, as he ran. *Thwomp. Thwomp. Thwomp.* Gasping, he stopped in front of his house and looked at the front door. The silhouettes of his parents displayed through the curtains. Their arms flailed about, heads bobbed to and fro. No doubt, they were fighting again. Arguing over dinner, the color of a chair, something trivial. Mike would certainly get the brunt of their frustration, one way or another.

Deciding to sneak through the back, he hobbled through the grass, and as he reached deeper into his jacket pocket, he felt a handful of pine needles. Darkness swallowed Lakewood as night fell. As he rounded the corner of the house, a hand grabbed his arm, pulled him into the shadows. Before he could react, he was fully embraced.

Before he could speak, her lips were pressed firmly against his. Jade's kiss calmed him.

She's okay, unharmed. He kissed her back, squeezed her tightly.

"Mike we're in trouble," she warned, still gripping his jacket with both hands.

"They know?"

"Yes. They know. They know it's us."

"How many of them? Do they all know?"

"They all know, Mike. *All* of them."

Mike exhaled, looked up, around, anywhere for a reasonable thought. Jade touched his face, directed his eyes into her own. "I have to get home. I heard the police are looking for me. My parents think I'm missing now, too." Faint, loud voices rattled the window that they stood next to. Jade saw his parents' argument affect her partner.

"Listen," she encouraged, "you're stronger than them." She hugged him again.

"Dealing with my parents is normal. I can take it," he guaranteed. "It's you I'm worried about. How much trouble are you going to be in? What are you going to tell your parents?"

The sensor on the yard light detected that the sun was almost down, the light began to illuminate.

"I'm just going to tell them I skipped school, take the punishment." Jade's face expressed hope. Used to being spoiled by her dad and stepmom, Jade banked on their soft punishment tonight. She pulled his hand, locked with hers, up and kissed the back of it.

"I'll tell you everything tomorrow. I need to get home and call off the search party." She smiled, hopeful, and ran through the back yard, the short way home.

Mike watched her leave, knowing how brave she had been today. If he could only just go home with her, help explain, keep her out of trouble. But he couldn't, not now. It would only further contaminate an already complex situation.

He opened the back door and knew it was going to be a long night. An empty bottle of liquor laid sideways on the coffee table, and a few drops of the drink pooled below the opening. His mother cried loudly; his father still yelled. He wished they would just divorce or at least send him away to a distant relative somewhere, anywhere. Sending him to a stranger would even be a relief.

He moved delicately to his room, closed the door. The smell of dinner drifting through the house teased his stomach. He was starving, but he'd wait. In a few hours, his dad would be passed out from the poisonous liquid that he had dedicated his life to. His mom would calm down, lose herself in front of some show about a lawyer, and speak out loud, to no one, about how foolish the woman on the show is to stay with her maniac husband. He could wander out then, warm a plate of whatever was left in the microwave.

He pulled the pine needles from his pocket, spread them out on his desk, under the reading lamp. He looked at them, wondering when it would be too late, what Jade saw today, and just how much time there was left.

*

Chief Jackson retired to his room early after receiving the call that Jade was now safe at home. He saved his questions for tomorrow, needing to process what he had seen at the hospital, to try and understand it.

Liz stayed quiet until she could hear her father's unmistakable snore creeping through the space under his bedroom door. In her PJs, hair pulled back in a ponytail, she entered her dad's study. Hundreds of books filled the shelves, colorful paintings hung on the walls, and piles of paperwork covered the desk.

She knew where to find what she wanted. She was still haunted by the look on her father's face when he left the hospital room where Giuseppe had passed. Being Chief of Police, her father was accustomed to seeing people in car accidents, other traumatic situations, but she'd never seen him with a look like that.

Terrified.

The door squeaked when she opened the lower portion of the cabinet. Her mom and dad used to share this office, but since her mother died last year, her dad had taken over the space, sliding most of her mother's things into the cabinets and drawers.

Liz found a binder, with *Sheila* hand-written in marker on the front. She hadn't seen her mother's name in a while. She unwound the string that held it closed, the accordion style folder popped open. The first item she found was a photograph of her mother. Sure, they still had family portraits hanging through the house, but this was different. It was candid, a snapshot. Something always seemed to get lost in an image taken at JCPenney where a photographer with five weeks experience positioned their chins, eyes, and shoulders into unnatural, sculptured poses.

This little piece of Kodak paper captured her mom's essence, her being. Sheila's eyes shined, her smile beamed. Liz smiled back at her, wishing for her embrace, remembering her smell, her perfume. She pulled random sheets of paper from the binder - wildlife material. Her mother loved animals, wanted to save the Rainforest, tigers, *moths*. She started a campaign to help preserve a species of moths in Lakewood that were dying off in great numbers.

Liz discovered another photo, a close-up, with a pine tree behind her mom, moths floating elegantly around her. She was beautiful, inside and out. Liz had her dimples, her cheeks, lips. Reaching in, she felt plastic, a bag.

She pulled it out and gasped, amazed at what her mother had stored inside. A Zip-Loc, yellow and blue make green, sealed sandwich bag filled with brown, dried pine needles. Liz's heart almost stopped beating.

Her mother, the woman who would fight to protect anything in need, might have been the one who needed protecting. Keeping the bag of needles and the picture of Sheila and the moths out, Liz put the papers back into the binder and placed it back into the cabinet.

She walked, thoughts scattered, back to her room, closed the door, and dialed the number to the phone in Iggy's bedroom.

Chapter 11

"Here," said Jade, acting bored, like her absence yesterday hadn't been something that put the entire school on high alert. The students, although having seen her walk into class after the bell in a noticeable *don't notice me* manner, turned their heads, synchronized, to stare at her.

Mr. Miller's eyes lifted from his attendance log, slow and cryptic. "Welcome, Jade. Glad to have you back, safe and sound."

She gawked at the teacher. Mike glanced back towards her, and Iggy and Liz both observed all of it.

Mr. Miller held his gaze, flinched, and then slapped his fingers to his cheek, holding them there. Jade watched, slumping in her seat, then pulled her long hair over her face, hiding her eyes. Mr. Miller pressed his cheek bone, firmly, massaging it in a circular motion.

The class watched, moved their eyes from Jade to Mr. Miller, catching the glances from the room in between. The bizarre silence broke when the teacher quickly smiled, closed his book, and stood up.

"It's *so* nice to have Jade back," he commented, then jerked his head to look at Mike.

Mike didn't look up, refused to give the teacher the treat of mouthing off or making a smart remark. He just sat, looking to his left at the pines through the window. Mr. Miller stared, relentlessly, begging Mike to react, to lose his cool. He didn't.

Mike waited him out, Mr. Miller began to conduct his lecture, disappointed.

*

The few cars that passed sent mist into the air from the wet street. The air outside was near freezing. Wondering how the fall leaves changed color and fell off seemingly overnight without him noticing, Chief Jackson looked at the bare trees that lined the street. Carried by a cool, gentle breeze, loose leaves passed by on the concrete, brushing over his shoes.

He pulled a small, leather kit from his back pocket and removed two long, squiggly wires from it. Dropping to one knee, Chief Jackson placed the wires into the keyhole on the front door of Greasy's, and wiggled them until he heard it click. With a twist of the knob, the door slowly creaked open.

The smell of marinara and parmesan cheese dominated the entire restaurant. With his flashlight, he searched for a switch, quickly found one. A single yellow light above the pool table dimly lit up Greasy's. It was quiet inside, cold, and still too dark to see much.

Scanning the area with squinted eyes, he struggled to see clearly. His thoughts of what might linger in the dark corners worried him. The image of boils contracting on Giuseppe's skin was seared into Jackson's mind. He had only seen such a thing once before and always prayed he never would again.

His steps echoed, and his black boots collected

dust from the filthy floor. When he reached the kitchen, the soft light from the lamp had lost its potency. He clicked his long, steel flashlight back on, shined it around the ovens and counters.

He crouched, one knee on the stained floor the other supporting his elbow. The beam from his battery powered torch inspected the corners where the walls met the floor. Dried bits of sausage, shriveled strands of mozzarella seemed right at home strewn around the entire space.

Giuseppe's housekeeping habits would make anyone cringe, but what Jackson saw next sent a shiver through him: pine needles.

Several of them, scattered about, inconspicuously trying to blend into Giuseppe's mess. The chief picked one up, smelled it, and snapped it in half. He stood, walked to the wooden door in the back of the kitchen.

Surprisingly, it was unlocked. He let himself into Giuseppe's office, flipped on the lamp atop the antique desk. Bills, bank statements partly filled out laid scattered. An old space heater on the floor, a rusty fan clipped above kept the pizza man comfortable as the calendar turned month by month.

Jackson tugged on the long drawer, the lamp wobbled on the quaking desk. He pulled again, jarring it loose. The wooden drawer made a rubbing sound, as it finally let go and slid out. So many pine needles filled the drawer, that some of them fell over the edge onto Jackson's feet when it popped open.

Seeing it filled to the brim, the chief shined his flashlight over them. Green and brown needles, hundreds of them, and... a glimmer. He selected a piece of unopened mail from the desktop and began to push the needles out of the drawer. Buried under an inch of needles, he found it.

It was so daunting, he needed to pause. He sat in the dead Italian's chair, filled with disbelief, and gathered himself.

*

The classroom had become so still, seconds could be

heard dropping from the wall clock down to the cheap tile floor. Liz counted seven ticks before Jade finally answered Principal Warren's question. "I'm fine," she grumbled.

Second period seemed to be off to the same bizarre start as first period. Only this time instead of Mr. Miller showing a strange interest in Jade's return, Principal Warren had interrupted Ms. Cain to question Jade.

Ms. Cain glugged raspberry yogurt off her plastic spoon, as the principal leaned over Jade, both his hands on her desk. His grin warm and welcoming. His eyes cold and distant. She folded her arms in protest and in self-protection and turned her head to gaze out the window at the pines. She could see her own and Principal Warren's faint reflections against the glass where beaded rain drops on the outside created a kaleidoscope of the two of them.

Liz felt herself shiver when he stood upright and turned away from Jade to deliver her a greeting.

"Good morning, Elizabeth," he said, with false delight. "I just got off the phone with your father. He's coming in today."

He sniffled and pressed his fingers against his right temple, furled his eyebrows. He appeared to fight off a sneeze. Liz wondered what was wrong with him until his bright, white teeth shined again with his returning smile. He turned and walked to the door, and Ms. Cain blushed when he shot a wink her direction.

Principal Warren marched down the lonely hall, designer shoes clicking on the shiny floor. The officer at the far end waited for the principal to approach, tried to give a nod and a good morning look, but Principal Warren looked right through him, beyond.

He reached out to his right, his hand touching the pad locks on the lockers, pulling each one and letting it fall back as he passed. Each one clinked against its locker, in synch with his slow clacking steps.

He rounded the corner leading to his office, finally giving the officer a quick glance, hardly acknowledging his *hello*.

Principal Warren's steps strolled on by, leaving the officer puzzled as the principal glided into his office and closed the door.

*

Iggy had his sights set on the furthest ball to the left. The one directly in front of Mike. Iggy was positioned to the far right, making the run to his target long. He'd have to be quick off the wall and burst forward when the whistle sounded. If he didn't, the task of running diagonally across the court could be suicide.

He could rely on the fact that many of the players on Mike's team will slightly pause, surprised by his move, slowing their sprints. But, should one of them keep his focus and go full speed ahead, Iggy could definitely be knocked out early, at the frontline of battle.

Knowing Mr. Armstrong's timing well Iggy felt he could guess the whistle and get a good jump. *Hold it, Iggy*, he thought to himself. *Not yet... not yet... not yet... now!*

He lunged forward, but after two steps he heard a whistle.

"False start!" yelled Mr. Armstrong. "Settle down, Sweetheart. One more of those and it's a DQ. Not talking about ice cream either, Princess."

Shoot! Not only was Iggy now just one misstep from disqualification, but he had also exposed his hand, tipped his pitch, revealed his strategy.

The gleam in Mike's eye was a combination of shock and delight, daring Iggy to try it again. His grin displayed confidence thinking that Iggy didn't have it in him to make another attempt. *Nice idea, but you blew it.* Iggy could practically read Mike's thoughts.

Iggy calmed himself, returned to the wall, and repositioned to wait for the whistle. These matches, battles, always played out the same. After a long, drawn out bloodbath, it always came down to Mike and Iggy, one on one. Mike was always able to outwit, out-perform, and deliver the game winner. That feeling, the ball bouncing off Iggy's body, was always terrible. Knowing Mike constantly won, that he himself couldn't stop him, haunted Iggy.

Right now, the way things were in Lakewood, the

way he couldn't get it right with Liz, Iggy wanted to beat Mike more than ever. Something had to give. Something had to change.

It is now, Iggy decided. This was the moment things would start to improve. He'd guess the whistle again and dart along on an angle. Sure, Mike knew what Iggy was planning on attempting, but would never expect him to be brave enough to try it a second time.

Iggy breathed slowly, into his nostrils out through his mouth. He relaxed, rocked forward on the balls of his feet, and then back. Forward, back. Forward, back. He knew he was fast enough. Successful execution relied only on a good start off the wall.

Calmly, Iggy anticipated the whistle. Waiting... Waiting... Waiting... *Now!*

He pressed firmly on his back foot, thrusted his weight forward! A split second before his sneaker sole left the gym floor with a squeak, he heard it – the whistle! He had timed it perfectly!

His strides were so smooth; he looked like a speed skater, gliding down the track. He was a blur, jetting across in front of the line of his teammates.

Mike couldn't believe what he was seeing and launched himself off his team's back wall towards the balls on the centerline. His legs were longer than Iggy's, and the distance he needed to cover was shorter. Both played to his advantage.

Iggy was a streak of determination, not fazed by Mike's long history of dominance. Two trucks heading for an intersection; two rams about to slam horns on a mountainside. Every player on both teams halted and watched their captains sprint at each other. Mr. Armstrong stared with his whistle hanging from the side of his mouth. Iggy, although always a fast runner, moved with new urgency!

They closed in on the centerline; the balls waited for them. The kids recognized the boys' renewed zealous battle. Cheers erupted through the gymnasium.

Iggy sprinted a half a step ahead. Now a full step! Now two steps! Iggy's angle allowed him to blast, full speed at the balls. Mike realized if he stayed at his own current speed, he wouldn't be able to stop. He'd cross the centerline and be out of the game before he could even grab a ball.

Iggy reached down with Mike just six feet away, picked up a ball and slung it, side arm from the hip. Mike made a spin move, trying to slip out of the ball's trajectory, but it was too late. The ball blasted a direct hit to his chest! Off balance, Mike's body made a complete turn, a three-sixty, as his legs gave out, unable to steady him.

He collapsed with a submissive thud, piled on the floor. *Defeated.*

Iggy's teammates exploded with pride behind him. Accomplished, he towered over Mike. Mike's team hung their heads, surprised, knowing without their leader, a loss was imminent. Mike lifted his head, inhaling the dirt and grime from the floor. Iggy had finally won. Finally overcome.

A lump formed in Mike's throat; his lungs burned. The one thing that he always had was stripped away. His dominance, erased. He breathed hard, feeling that all he was now is a kid who hated his school, hated his home, hated everything. A kid that not only his teachers despised, but his parents too. Iggy's proud stance turned blurry in Mike's watery eyes.

He couldn't lose to Igor Andrews. Not now.

Not ever.

*

"Can anyone tell me which state produces the most yogurt?" Ms. Cain's question was directed at nobody in particular. Even she knew that not one single kid in the classroom was actually listening to her. "It's New York. Isn't that wonderful?"

Liz watched Jade's fingers, covered with silver lead dust, grip her number two pencil. It made a scratching sound, left traces of the image in Jade's mind on the blue-lined, white paper. Trees. Evergreens. Pines with hollow eye sockets, staring out of the page at her. In the middle stood a small tree, cowering under the giants that surrounded it.

"New York is one of the country's largest

producers of dairy. It's not all Wall Street stocks and bonds, children. Dairy. Lots of dairy." Ms. Cain continued her senseless babble. "Everyone knows yogurt has important probiotics. But, did you know it can also effectively battle acid reflux?"

The lead on Jade's pencil snapped. "Do you think anyone cares about this?" she complained with fire in her voice.

Ms. Cain's eyes doubled in size. "Excuse me?"

Jade spoke loud, clear, strongly enunciating each syllable, "I don't give a crap about yogurt."

After Jade's aggressive tone, Ms. Cain fumbled her words, "Well, Jade… Just w-what is it that *you* care about?"

The girl's gaze pierced the teacher's skin. Malevolently, she sat up straight, "The pine needles under your desk. *That's* what I care about."

Ms. Cain put her hand on her cheek, holding it like she was putting pressure on a cut. Gritting her teeth, she looked down on the floor below her desk. Liz was paying close attention, not sure what was happening. Jade slowly looked away from the angry teacher and started sketching again.

*

Mike struck while Iggy was turned away, facing the adoring applause of his teammates. Up off the floor with lightning speed, Mike plowed into Iggy's back.

They crashed ferociously to the hardwood. Mike landed a punch to Iggy's ribs, but Iggy quickly spun under him, and jabbed his knee into Mike's stomach.

The surrounding cheers had turned to gasps, hollers. Both teams charged, forming a barrier around the two grappling students. Faces red, hair askew, the two boys tumbled around. Iggy was on top, then Mike. Both fighters were doing damage. Knuckles on cheeks, jaws, eyes. Mr. Armstrong shrieked, commanding a ceasefire, but no one could hear him over the chants.

He pushed his way through, saw Iggy land a fierce blow to Mike's nose. Blood splattered across the floor. Mike retaliated with a punch to Iggy's mouth, splitting his lips wide open, knocking Iggy backwards and off of him.

Mr. Armstrong jumped between them, but Mike forced his way past the coach, through him. Down they went again! Mike had Iggy's shirt gripped in both fists, pinning him down. Iggy tried to free himself and force Mike off, but he wasn't strong enough. Mr. Armstrong rammed into them, breaking Mike's hold.

The onlookers yelled with delight; a fight of this magnitude had not occurred at Lakewood Pines for quite some time. Finally, a few students from each team restrained the boys, holding them by the arms. Iggy lunged at Mike again, but he was weak, breathing heavy. Mike, too, tried to reach Iggy but hadn't the strength to get free from his captors.

Iggy's ears rang from the punches Mike had landed to the side of his face. He could hardly hear Mr. Armstrong's muffled voice over the buzzing sound. He saw blood, running down Mike's chin, forming puddles on the floor and staining his shirt.

With a kid on each of their arms, they were

escorted, like prisoners of war, behind Mr. Armstrong who led the way. Their bodies were sore, bruised. Their hands were swollen even more than their faces. Like criminals being taken to jail after sentencing, they were dragged down the hallway. Kids from inside classrooms cranked their necks to get a glimpse of the bloodied combatants as they noisily passed through the halls.

Mr. Armstrong lectured angrily the length of the long, cemented corridor. His voice bounced from side to side, but never found Iggy's ears.

The new dodge ball champion just looked straight ahead. Beating Mike at dodgeball felt good, pummeling Mike felt even better. He wished they hadn't been stopped, interrupted. He looked at Mike from the corner of his swollen eye, wanting to attack again, but resisted the urge, knowing he was already in quite deep.

The gym teacher shoved the boys into Principal Warren's office. The principal viewed the battered fighters and smirked.

"These two need to see you," Mr. Armstrong announced, puffing from the excitement.

"Sit down," Principal Warren demanded. He gave Mr. Armstrong a nodding gesture, signaling him to leave and to shut the door behind him.

Sissy Daniels peeked over the principal's shoulder at Mike and Iggy from the *MISSING* poster on the back wall of the office. A small potted sapling sat on the corner of Warren's expensive, black desk. Pine needles laid around it on the sleek, polished finish.

Principal Warren smiled, leaned back, hands folded on his stomach. "What's the problem, fellas," he questioned. "Fighting, are we?"

Neither of them answered.

"The blood on your faces?" he pointed, "What happened?"

Paying no attention to the man questioning them, Mike stared at the tiny pine tree on the desk.

"I know what happened to the girl," Iggy said, motioning to the poster with his eyes.

Principal Warren turned back and looked at her picture. Facing Iggy again, he widened his eyes and raised his brows curiously. "Sissy? You know what happened to her?"

Iggy nodded.

"By all means," the principal leaned forward, "tell me."

Iggy looked at Mike, still concentrating on the tree, focused. "Mike did something to her," he said.

Blank faced, Mike barely reacted, turned and looked at Iggy.

Principal Warren's mouth developed a slow grin, until his right eye squeezed shut. He pinched it, tightly, closed. He pressed his middle finger against his temple, stretched his jaw, popping it. His grin casually returned. "It's actually quite, um, good that the two of you are here."

Iggy raised his eyebrows, Mike stared only at the small pine tree in the pot on the principal's desk.

"There's someone here to see you," Warren said, "Both of you." He pressed a button on his desk phone, spoke into it, "Please, send Chief Jackson in."

Okay, Principal Warren. Right away. The woman's cheerful voice replied covered with static.

"Thank you," he said, sitting back, rocking in his leather chair.

Confused, Iggy looked back at the door, seeing Liz's father enter. Mike still did not break his deep study of the tree.

"Principal Warren," Jackson said, lacking enthusiasm. Warren just smiled, continued to rock.

"What's going on here?" Iggy asked, standing up. "Mr. Jackson, I think I know what happened to that girl. To Sissy."

Chief Jackson looked at him, "I need you boys to come with me. To the station."

"What is this about?" Iggy raised his voice.

"Mike, come with us, please."

Mike got out of his seat, locked eyes with the principal, until he was ushered out of the office. Chief Jackson touched Iggy's shoulder, indicated with his eyes that Iggy had no choice but to obey.

"Dad," Liz's voice greeted them in the school office lobby, "Don't do this!"

"Liz, why aren't you in class?" her father asked.

"I saw your patrol car pull up," her voice cracked. "Don't take him!"

"Go back to class, Dear," the chief told her, calmly.

"Dad, no!"

He snapped severely, "Liz, *enough*."

She frantically grabbed her father's arm. "Dad, no!"

He looked at the officer that was with him and nodded. The man clutched Liz, holding her back. She ripped herself away, pressed against Iggy, gripped his face with her hands, and slammed her lips against his. Her mouth, soft, clung to him. Iggy's body tingled, melted into gelatin.

Abruptly, the officer snatched her away. Her eyes held tightly to Iggy, until he was outside, being loaded into the back of the police car with Mike Lawman.

Chapter 12

Thursday – 11:13 am

"Sit down," Chief Jackson demanded, dropping himself into his chair impatiently.

"Are we under arrest?" Mike asked, anxiously.

"Just sit down." The chief pointed at the two folding chairs across from him. Mike stood tall. Iggy sat down cooperatively. Chief Jackson rolled his eyes at the defiant one. "No, you're not under arrest. Not yet, anyway."

"What the hell is this about?" Mike demanded information. "We have rights, you know?"

"Would you like me to read them to you? Put the cuffs on you? Book you?"

Mike sat down next to Iggy, sensing Chief Jackson just might do what he threatened. The chief took a long swig from his mug as steam drifted up from the hot coffee.

"Mr. Jackson, what are we doing here?" Iggy tiptoed with his voice, twiddled his thumbs.

Chief Jackson opened his desk drawer and slammed a clear, plastic bag down in front of them. It contained a very familiar item. Iggy retreated to a slouch, surprised to see it. Mike didn't react at all.

"See this?" Jackson asked. "Have you seen this before?" He rested his elbows on the desk. "Before you answer, let me inform you about something. Iggy, on the night that one of my officers chased you through the park- -yes we know it was you--the dash camera in his patrol car caught someone throwing something that looked an awful lot like this into a dumpster in front of the bank."

Iggy's throat dried up, like the Sahara. His seat suddenly grew firm, uncomfortable. He squirmed, looking for some relief but found none.

"And may I also tell you that we've dusted it. We've found two clearly identifiable sets of prints on it. One belongs to Sissy Daniels, the other to you, Mike."

Mike showed no surprise. He sat stone cold, statue-like. He remembered being fingerprinted last year when he got into trouble for vandalizing some mailboxes. His prints were on file, and they had made the match.

"Mr. and Mrs. Daniels have confirmed that this necklace belongs to Sissy. How or why it ended up in Giuseppe's desk at Greasy's is beyond me. I can't tell you why, but that man always seemed to have his finger on the pulse of whatever bizarre thing happens to be going on in Lakewood. All I know is, someone needs to start talking. Now." The gold chain with a dove pendant sat on the desk between the boys and Chief Jackson.

After about sixty seconds of total silence, Iggy started to sputter something random.

Immediately, Mike snapped from his coma and cut him off. "We're not saying a word," he blurted. "Not without our parents. And a lawyer."

Chief Jackson sighed, knowing he couldn't force them to talk without their legal guardians. "Okay, go sit in the lobby. I'll make some calls."

*

"Hey, Lizard. Can I come in?" Jade's voice was calm but resolute. Liz had been pacing, mad at her father, upset with Lakewood, the world. Jade had never knocked on Liz's door before. Only a birthday party in first grade brought her there once. Curious, Liz promptly let her in. They sat alone in the kitchen across from each other at the table. Liz had never just up and left school in the middle of the day like that, and she figured that Jade probably hadn't either.

Yet, there they were, together.

Jade leaned forward and declared bluntly. "We need to talk."

Liz forcefully asked, "You and Mike are a couple. Right?"

That was not why Jade came over, but it was a fair place to start. "Yeah, we are."

"Why all the sneaking? Why do you hide it?"

Jade shrugged, "It works. Hiding it. It's no secret that no one likes me much. No one cares much."

~

"It's no one's business anyway," Mike explained to Iggy, as they sat unattended in the Police Station lobby, waiting for Chief Jackson to call their homes.

"You think you'll hurt your image if someone finds out?" Iggy asked with raised eyebrows and a smirk.

"My image? Seriously? My image is that I'm a troublemaker. How could Jade hurt that?"

"Good point."

Mike looked at Iggy, "People don't like me anyway. What do I care?"

~

"No offense, Jade, but if no one likes you it's because of how you act. You know, all mysterious like, strange and weird," Liz told her.

"I don't like people. Almost no one," Jade conceded. "I want people to stay away from me. Avoid me. Think that I'm up to something."

~

"*Are* you up to something, Mike?" Iggy pried.

"Maybe." Mike thought silently for a moment.

"Maybe I am, Igor."

~

Jade slouched. "Mike gets me. People wouldn't get Mike getting me, so it's easier to pretend we don't even know each other. It's not like you and Iggy."

~

"You and Liz have it made," Mike touted.

It sounded good to hear *you and Liz.* Iggy's heart leaped. "Well, we may have to start hiding things soon, too."

"What do you mean?"

Iggy looked around the room. "Her dad just brought me into the police station, man."

Mike smiled, acknowledged Iggy's point.

~

"My dad doesn't like Iggy anymore," Liz explained to her. Jade laughed at the thought.

Liz gave a forceful look, determined, "Did you guys do something to that girl? Sissy?"

Jade's smile disintegrated. "I came here to talk about that girl."

~

"What happened to her?" Iggy wondered.

Mike just pondered him. Hollow and evasive at first, he then relaxed. "I guess I have to tell you. We're almost out of time."

~

"Mike and I had a great summer. Sneaking around, meeting in the middle of the night. Being a secret, falling in love." Jade blushed when she spoke.

~

"I'm touched," Iggy mocked him.

"Hey, you're not the only one who has feelings you know," Mike said, hiding slight embarrassment. "We just get along. It's nice."

~

"We would meet up in the pines. A lot," Jade continued. "Last Saturday, the pines was our spot to meet again." She lifted her chin up, eyes filled with a dreamy glaze, remembering the romance she felt that night. "We walked, holding hands, talking. Mike can talk for hours. He's so sweet and kind."

Liz interrupted, "Get to the point."

~

"I mean, you sound so... so strange right now," Iggy said. "Is this the same Mike that wants to kill me during dodgeball?"

"Don't sound so surprised," Mike said, "I have to be that way when we're competing. Or I'd never beat you."

Iggy waited before starting again, "So you met in the pines that night?"

~

"The way Mike kissed me that night was different. Amazing," Jade closed her eyes, reminiscing. "I almost floated away, Lizard."

~

"What about the girl?" Iggy pressed. "Where does she fit in this story?"

"We had been hearing something," Mike described, "like someone following us. I caught a glimpse of a person. A girl."

"Sissy Daniels?"

~

Jade nodded.

"What happened next?" Liz raised off her seat, anxious to finally hear the truth.

"She walked into a thick group of trees, and we lost track of her. I thought she was hiding from us. After a few minutes, we heard her scream." Jade paused.

"She screamed. Lights flashed from the pines. Deep in the pines. Liz, she was in pain. Terrible agony. I could hear it in her voice." Jade covered her face with her hands, frightened by the memory.

Liz moved closer, touched Jade's shoulder. "It's okay. What next? What happened?"

~

Mike took a deep breath before continuing. "Jade and I searched for her. For hours, we looked. We couldn't find anything... except that necklace. It was hanging on a small pine tree. A tree no taller than either of us."

"Why haven't you told the police? The teachers? Anyone?" Iggy tried to keep his voice down, but instead it cracked and shot down the hallway. He exhaled and settled himself down hoping he hadn't been overheard.

~

Jade looked up at Liz. "You have to believe me. What I'm about to tell you."

Liz sat back down, across from her, braced herself. "Okay," she said eagerly.

"We saw Principal Warren that night, just outside of the pines. He told us to go home. He yelled."

"And?"

Jade swallowed. "We were scared."

~

"We didn't think anyone would believe us," Mike explained. "But, then we went back the following night."

"You did?"

"Yeah, we did."

~

"We saw them," Jade said, "We saw all of them."

"All of who?" Liz stood up from the excitement.

"Principal Warren, Mr. Miller, Mr. Armstrong, Ms. Cain. There may be more, but we hope not." She buried her face again.

~

"The lights were so bright, Igor. The wind, the screaming," Mike slumped over.

"What were they doing?" Iggy's heart pounded fiercely against his sternum.

~

"Changing," Jade mumbled, tears starting to form in her eyes. "They were *changing.*" Jade breathed out the words in a ghostly whisper.

~

"Giuseppe knew things. He lived by the pines. He saw things. The pines made him sick," Mike leaned in, inches from Iggy's face. "They killed him."

~

"Liz," Jade whispered, "Your mom knew things. She found out about them while she was in the woods. They made her sick. They killed her."

~

Iggy sat still, digesting all that Mike had told him. All he could think about were pine needles everywhere. The two of them were startled by three officers sprinting from the main office.

"Clear the way! Look out!" one of them yelled, sprinting to Jackson's office. Others followed them.

"Get an ambulance!" a voice screamed from inside. "Get an ambulance now!"

*

"I guess I was wrong," Mike admitted, more to himself than to any of the others.

The four kids were in front of Jackson's hospital bed, Liz paced, frantically. "What do you mean?" Iggy asked, eyes on his panicking girlfriend.

"We thought maybe Chief Jackson was one of them," Jade answered for Mike.

"*Where were you?* Yesterday?" Liz demanded loudly, voice cracking. "When you weren't at school."

"I left Jade in the pines," Mike explained. "She was looking for the girl, clues, anything."

"And?" Iggy blurted out.

"It's a lot of things, Iggy," Jade told them.

"Things we found out about them and the girl's disappearance. What Giuseppe had was helpful."

"Your mother was helpful, Liz," Mike added.

"What are you talking about?" Liz and Iggy asked in harmony.

"Giuseppe and your mom were investigating the pines. Trying to figure out the secrets. The mystery," Jade informed.

"There's information at Greasy's. Documents recording their work," Mike said, while Chief Jackson laid still, hooked up to monitors and medicine.

Iggy looked at Liz; she touched his arm. A physical *it's okay.* "I found pine needles in my mom's things. Is that why she had them?"

Jade nodded.

"What's wrong with my father?" Liz asked, looking at the chief, helplessly asleep. Nurses rushed by the open door, prompting Mike to close it.

"Your mother was too close. Giuseppe was too close. Now your dad is." Jade's voice was low. Her eyes averted to the floor.

Liz sniffled and pretended her eyes weren't filling with tears, Iggy wrapped his arm around her.

"So, he's going to die?" Liz concluded through her swollen throat.

"How do you know all this?" Iggy's disbelief seeped from his lips.

"We told you," Mike reassured, "It's all at Greasy's. The way they work, what they do. They can put this, this illness inside of people."

"Who?!" Iggy asked, feeling overwhelmed with this newfound information.

"*Them.* Warren, the teachers," Mike reiterated.

"Poison?" Iggy whispered.

"We don't know for sure, but we don't think it is poison," Jade told him.

"Why are you two not ill then? Why aren't you two both sick? In a hospital bed?" Liz questioned confused and unsure what to believe anymore.

Sensing Iggy and Liz's doubt, Mike answered calmly. "They don't want to kill us," he said.

"What then? Huh?" Iggy was getting anxious.

Liz's head rested on his shoulder.

Jade stepped closer, eye to eye with Liz. "They want to *grow* us, Lizard."

Chapter 13

Thursday – 4:44 pm

What a day, Iggy thought. A fight at school, being questioned at the police office, Liz's father was maybe dying in the hospital, and now this; sneaking through a filthy alley behind what was quickly becoming the world's most mysterious pizza shop. He, Liz, and Jade stood behind Mike.

Iggy's eyes grew large, looking around, paranoid.

"Where did you get that key?" he asked Mike, who had just unlocked the back door of Greasy's from the back alley. The door that entered directly into Giuseppe's office.

"Jade found it," Mike answered casually.

"Found it *where?*" Iggy grabbed the cuff of Mike's jacket.

"Giuseppe's house," Jade answered, composed.

"How did you get into his house?" Iggy nervously asked as he turned his head quickly to the girl. He, hesitant and apprehensive, knew a bad situation when he was in one, and he was in one now.

"Broke a window," she said, casually.

"Jade made good use of her time yesterday," Mike bragged with a smirk.

The back alley was empty, except for some trash cans, stained pizza boxes piled close to the wall. No cars passing, no people, no eyes. Just the four of them, catching drizzle on their hair.

"Come on," Mike suggested hurriedly. "Someone might come along and see us."

Iggy, unsure, paused, but Liz stepped forward, entering. He was not about to let her go in there alone with the leading suspect in the disappearance of Sissy Daniels. He followed her, making sure Mike could see the seriousness in his stare. *Don't even think about hurting her.*

Jade flipped on the desk lamp. They could see the

pine needle filled drawer where Chief Jackson had found the necklace.

Jade shrugged her shoulders at Mike: *I missed it.*

He raised his eyebrows: *No big deal.*

She moved the space heater that sat near her feet and revealed a fire safe. Squatting down, she pressed four of the numbers. *Beep. Beep. Beep. Beep. Click.* It unlocked.

"Where did you get the code for that?" Iggy inquired.

Jade didn't look up, just dug what she was looking for out of the safe. She then turned the space heater around, pointed at the yellow Post-it note stuck to the back. *0-7-1-0.*

"July tenth," Liz said remembering how that date used to be celebrated every year growing up.

"What?" Iggy wondered what she was talking about.

She pointed. "The code. Zero-seven-one-zero. It's *seven-ten.* July tenth. My mom's birthday. She set the code on that safe. I guarantee, she did."

Jade stood up after pulling something from the safe. "You ready for this, Lizard?" She reached out, handing her a folder filled with papers, photos, and, most importantly, a scent. The perfume Liz's mother used to make in the garage - *Forevergreen.* Iggy smelled it, too.

Liz's eyes lit up. "Take a look," said Jade with soft eagerness.

Liz wiped the pine needles off the desktop and sat in the dead pizza man's chair. When she opened the folder, Forevergreen filled the room like sunlight at the crack of dawn.

The lamp shined on a photograph of pine trees. A pointing hand entered the frame from the right side, and the fourth finger exhibited a ring: Sheila Jackson's wedding ring. Liz would recognize the yellow gold band and round cut diamond anywhere.

She picked up the picture, and stacked underneath it were samples of pine needles preserved between glass microscope slides, and pages of notes. Giuseppe's and Sheila's compiled and organized research in detail.

One page in her mother's perfect cursive

handwriting read:

Apparently, the experiment is going well. Giuseppe's usually strong reaction when entering the pines, seemed much calmer today. It's amazing to think that we just might be there. We just might be solving this baffling mystery. We've been able to pinpoint a few of the members, but we still don't know exactly why they are here or who their leader is.

Another page read:

I went to the school today to visit Elizabeth's principal. While informing Principal Warren that I would be conducting tests in the pines (of course I told him it pertained to the moths), something bizarre happened. He became ill. Physically ill right before my eyes. Cold sweats, heavy breathing, muscle spasms. He repeatedly covered his face with a handkerchief while gagging uncontrollably. Could it really be? I suppose it's possible.

The words flew off the pages into Liz, through her, confusing her. What was her mother talking about? She and Iggy flipped through dozens of entries, shaking their heads, looking at one another, still unsure of exactly what was going on.

I developed the pictures from Monday and brought them along with me into the pines. Giuseppe stayed behind, so we can conserve our resources. I can now say that I am completely positive that some of the trees in the pines are not in the same location as they were when I took these pictures. Explain it? I can't. All I know is that a few of these tall, ominous trees that must be seventy or eighty years old are... moving. There I said it. As confusing as it is, I believe this brings us one step closer to solving this mystery.

"What is this all about?" Iggy asked puzzled, looking up from the journal. "What is she writing about?"

Jade and Mike shared a confident glance.

Jade turned several pages of the journal to one

with an image. "This is what it's all about," she said decisively, pushing the page towards them.

Iggy and Liz couldn't believe what they were seeing, but now all the terminology was making sense to them. *Trees moving. They want to grow us.*

All four kids studied that picture and other images. It was terrifying to see, nightmarish. It was inconceivable. The back of the journal was written by Giuseppe. Iggy and Liz were so entranced and enticed by the information they couldn't read the Italian's words fast enough.

Their power is strong, but maybe not strong enough to stay completely under control. At night, it seems, they change. They make their way to the pines and begin their transformation. They hurry to the trees. I've heard them talking through my hidden mics in the pizza shop. I hear so much that way. A transformation outside of the pines would result in a permanent state. It would trap them, stop them.

Liz flipped the page.

Since Sheila's passing, my research has been much more difficult. I can't get deep enough into the pines to achieve anything. Without her experimentation, I don't have access to the pines anymore. I have nothing to protect myself. She planned on letting her husband know about all this evil, or at least try to. Last year, his reaction was strongly negative, jam-packed with contention. I don't blame him. Had I not seen it for myself, I would've thought she was crazy, too. Either way, I'm in trouble. If they were able to get rid of her, I will certainly be next.

The final entry was dated last Sunday. The day after Sissy Daniels went missing.

Their plan has been implemented. They've started with a child that is new to town. This will probably keep the other students from becoming frantic while they test it on her. The initial experiment worked. I'm amazed, but it worked. Her transformation was quick. After it happened, I tried to get to her. I would have saved her if I could have. They're being smart about it, too. I spoke to Chief Jackson, briefly, but if his own wife couldn't convince him, how will I? Soon, not a child in Lakewood will be safe.

Chapter 14

Thursday – 8:46 pm

Liz observed her father's chest move with each breath he took. His eyes, closed, wiggled under his eyelids, left and right. A handful of pine needles were scattered around the floor. She picked one off his blanket and felt sickened and scared that his illness was so similar to Giuseppe's.

Had her mother's passing been of the same horrible nature? Only now did she realize how little she actually knew of the sickness that took her mom away. The room was cold, damp feeling. Her father shivered on the bed next to where she stood but he seemed a million miles away from her.

"My aunt and uncle said you're more than welcome to stay with us tonight," Iggy gently offered, walking in behind her.

"Look at the needles," she said in awe. "They're just… here." She quickly plucked several more off the wool blanket. Liz turned and stomped the black pedal on the stainless-steel trash can in the corner of the room, slammed the needles into it wishing that somehow it would inflict pain on those responsible for her father's condition.

"Whatever your mother was trying to prevent before she died is now happening." Iggy said.

"Why didn't she tell us? Tell somebody?" Liz asked desperately, knowing Iggy couldn't possibly know the answer.

"Maybe we were all safer not knowing," he speculated, attempting to ease her wonder. "How much do you think your father knows?"

"It seems not much. Or at least he didn't believe it," she assumed. "He knew something though. I saw his face when Giuseppe died. He was scared, like he'd seen it before."

"Your mom."

"Yeah…"

"It must be how she died," Iggy concluded. Liz didn't respond, didn't look up.

"Your dad's not going to die, Liz. We'll save him. Somehow."

"You should have heard Giuseppe screaming, Iggy." She remembered vividly the chilling cry he let out at the end of his life.

"That's not going to be your dad. I promise."

"I can't lose him, too," she choked, wiping her moist eyes.

Softly, he put his arm around her quaking shoulder. The sound of something small hitting the hard, linoleum floor caught Iggy's attention. Hearing it again, he squatted down. He found pine needles falling from under the bed to the floor.

"Liz… look at this," he called, amazed.

She kneeled and joined him, equally stunned by the sight. Every few seconds another one dropped to the floor and laid carelessly, like it was not the strangest thing in the world. Liz jumped up and wailed when she looked back at her father.

Terrified, she pointed at the bed. Iggy quickly stood, grabbed her in his arms. He wanted to scream too, when he saw it. Chief Jackson's blanket was covered in pine needles. Out of nowhere, they had appeared on him.

Iggy flailed his hands, knocking the needles off Liz's dad. She joined in the effort, but with every swipe, more returned. The floor was now covered with the prickly, green needles.

She brushed them off hysterically until Iggy finally wrapped his arm around her waist and pulled her into the hallway, struggling. She fought to get back inside, but he blocked her, grabbing her shoulders.

"Stop!" he yelled.

"I'm not leaving!" she insisted. "I'm *not* leaving."

"Calm down, we can figure this out," he assured her. "Mike and Jade have found a lot of good evidence. We can figure this out."

"It'll be too late," her voice cracked, "He'll die!"

Passing nurses stopped, noticing the commotion between the two pre-teens.

"We're fine," Iggy notified them with a stressful influx in his awkwardly maturing voice. When the concerned nurses continued to stare he said it again, this time calmly and with a fake smile, "We're fine."

They looked to Liz for confirmation of the boy's claim. "We're okay," she whispered. "Sorry we raised our voices."

The nurses hesitantly left the two of them and continued their evening rounds.

"Liz, let's go home."

"I'm not going, Iggy," she reiterated, "I'm staying here. I'll sleep in the room with him."

"In there?" Iggy questioned her loudly with disbelief and overwhelming concern, then looked for the nurses, but luckily, they didn't come that time. "In *there?*" he said, this time much softer.

She nodded.

"Liz, something is going on in there. Something bad."

"Okay, I'll sleep in the waiting room." She was *not* leaving. Her mind was made up.

Iggy refused to fight her on this. He had lost both of his parents and could only imagine how it would have been to see them in this condition before it happened.

"I have to check in at home with my Aunt and Uncle," he told her. She nodded at him, understanding he would stay if he could. He raised his eyebrows, winked. She was tough, always had been. If anyone he knew could handle this, it was her. He kissed her lips, pressed his forehead against hers, she embraced him. Iggy turned when she loosened her grip, started down the hall.

"Iggy," she called out to him. He spun, hoping she had changed her mind, but that wasn't why she stopped him.

"I love you," she said. "I love you, Iggy."

"I love you too, Liz," he replied, knowing that it was true, that deep down no one could ever be to him what she was.

*

Unable to sleep, Liz tossed and turned again. Apparently,

those waiting for loved ones to come out of surgery or recover from illness, or an accident, spent more time pacing the floor than sitting on the furniture. The carpet was worn, and the sofa in the waiting room was stiff, hardly used. Enough light from the hallway sneaked in to reveal that the wall clock displayed just after midnight.

Losing her father now seemed impossible for Liz to handle. When her mother died, she thought nothing could be worse, but at least she still had her dad. He stepped up, in Sheila's absence, becoming both mom *and* dad. Although still learning the role of a mom, he was somewhat of a natural. Even when he wasn't fair, particularly lately with Iggy, he still loved Liz above all else. How could she carry on without him now?

She sat up and tied her shoelaces. Double knots, tight, secure enough to stay even when running. She grabbed her jacket and slipped out past the nurse's station.

Getting past the hospital's security guard wasn't difficult for her. She was swift, could move like a phantom. Coldness chilled the air and formed ice on the wet sidewalks. Most yards were buried with fallen brown leaves. The only color anywhere was the variation of hues on the shrubs that lined the walkways and the scattered pine trees around town. The evergreens.

She creeped down the creaky wooden stairs of her home's basement. It was dusty and gloomy down there. The basement served mainly as a room only to hold the home's vital organs: water heater, furnace, and breaker box. The heart and soul.

On the shelves, however, there were some other things. Boxes and random items. Along the floor mice traps and spider webs intertwined, and the block walls featured stains of water damage.

Cardboard boxes, labeled with black permanent marker, hugged the back wall on the multi-layered shelf. Liz surveyed them with her eyes, remembering. Rifling through Christmas decorations and rummaging through toys with plastic buttons that lit up and played music that serenaded her, Liz could hear her childhood.

The high-pitched melodies of nursery rhymes haunted her; her mom came to life in her heart with each box she opened. She found a painting she made her dad for Father's Day in second grade. She grinned at the lack of detail and at the memory of how wonderful he thought it was. *My little princess made this for me?*

Liz's hand brushed over books she read at bedtime that sent her imagination soaring just in time for dreaming. She uncovered clothing that she had outgrown, outfits that she had worn to school and church. *Oh, Mom, here's the pink dress with the white fur collar I wore to Auntie Bev's wedding.*

Her entire happy life with her parents was seemingly boxed and preserved. That life she no longer knew felt so long ago. How could it have only been a year ago?

Her throat tickled from the mildew in the musty, stagnant air. It tasted old. Older than her, probably. With no circulation, this could be the same air that went in and out of her mother's lungs when she was down here, packing away the items they no longer needed.

Liz blew a cobweb from her face and shivered from its tickle. The further to the left she went, the newer the items got. It was a chronological history of her family.

From baby clothes to outdated video game consoles. If archeologists one hundred years from now found these boxes, they could pinpoint major events, time frames, fashions, trends.

Most of all, they'd know when Sheila died. There at the end of the shelf were the boxes with Liz's mom's name on them. The suddenly large collection of the things *Sheila* no longer needed. All of her things, together in one place.

Liz pulled open the folded lid on the first box, found clothes. Mom's clothes. Liz could remember her in each outfit, looking smashing and perfect. Sniffling and her nose running, Liz lifted the lid of the next box: jewelry, her mom's purse, and a wallet. All the things that her mom picked out one day while in the mall or department store.

Pulling the next box open, a tired and worn down Liz abruptly stopped. Her heart thumped, heavily. She jerked her hand to her mouth, and a sudden burst of energy flew through her exhausted body.

She had done it. She found it, or it had found her.

She inhaled deeply, confidently. The magical wonders of deep understanding. An extraordinary, spine-tingling gift from her mom.

It was *Forevergreen.*

*

With her hands in the large, front pouch of her hooded sweatshirt, mist freezing on her hair, Liz stood in Iggy's backyard filled with determination and excitement. The items in her backpack rattled together when she tossed a pinecone up at Iggy's bedroom window. Only seconds after it hit, his light turned on. She watched, as he slid the window open.

"Were you already awake?" she asked, eyes happy to see him.

"Yup. Couldn't sleep if I tried."

"Get dressed and get down here," she motioned with her hand. "I've got something to show you."

"Way ahead of you," he slung his leg out through the open window. "I knew you'd be coming. I'm all dressed and ready to go."

Her face blushed, as she watched him descend down the side of the house. When his feet hit the grass, she wrapped her arms around his neck, kissed him. With confidence, he grabbed her hand, locked fingers with her.

They were back together. It was official. Fingers intertwined and kissing is how it used to be. How it *should* be. They didn't say much; their shoes clopped on the sidewalk.

Alert, they looked for patrol cars or anyone else. She didn't have to tell him where they were going; he already knew. The hospital. Where else?

Approaching the parking lot, they crouched low in the shrubs, taking stock of the situation before sneaking to the door. A hospital security guard stood near the entrance, but he wouldn't stay there long. He had a route, a circular pattern he made around the property.

They also saw a police squad car in the lot. No doubt, an officer was there to check up on the chief.

Iggy pointed, seeing the officer walking up the brightly lit parking lot. The cop gave the security guard a quick *hello, how are ya'* and entered through the automatic door. The kids held still, side by side, waiting in the damp bushes.

The guard, bored, accustomed to non-eventful nights on duty, nonchalantly wandered around the far corner of the building for a smoke. Liz and Iggy exchanged a glance. Him walking away from the entrance was all they needed. Sprinting across the blacktop, hand in hand, they looked only straight ahead at the front entrance.

They slipped through, quickly darted to the right into an alcove filled with magazines and pamphlets about flu shots and other illness preventions.

Hospitals were never empty, but the one in Lakewood, at that time of night was close to it. No receptionists, no greeters, no visitors. Still attached at the palms, Iggy and Liz had the same thought. They poked their eyes around the corner, saw no one, and rushed across to the door leading to the stairs.

A squeak from the metal hinges reverberated, and the door clicked shut behind them. Liz turned to say something when they heard a door again, only this time it was the door above them on the second floor. They scurried to the corner between a garbage can and the railing.

A man's shuffling feet rushed across the landing overhead and began descending the flight of stairs. The two seventh-graders held their breaths, knowing he would pass just inches from them.

When the man reached the middle landing where the stairway changed direction, Liz and Iggy got a clear look at him. The officer they saw in the parking lot held something, a magazine. Probably one he picked up in the lobby. The air between the kids and the officer gripped Liz's hair like a ghost's hand, moving it slightly. She held her breath and waited until the door clicked shut behind him.

Quickly, on their toes, keeping their steps light, they glided up the staircase and sneaked through to the second floor. Like downstairs, this floor was in a quiet nighttime routine. A janitor mopped the long hall to the right with his back to them. A young, blond woman at the nurse's station sat, occupied by the monitors and computer screen.

If they stayed low, crouched, they could slip below her line of sight, should she look up. The tranquil building required ninja style execution, patience, and a crafty skill earned by years of sneaking out of bedroom windows to rendezvous at the swing set.

The two experts creeped past her, completely unnoticed. Looking left and right, they slithered into Chief Jackson's room, closing and locking the door.

The smell of pine needles assaulted them so strongly, it stole their breaths. Liz shielded her eyes when Iggy pulled back the curtain that surrounded the bed. The site was more than they anticipated, worse than they imagined. The chief's skin glistened, covered in a thick coating of a sticky, cream-like substance.

Pine sap.

Iggy scraped his foot back and forth on the floor, watched the toe of his sneaker push around the pine needles. They were everywhere. The floor, Jackson's blanket, even a few small, red and swollen pimples on the chief's face appeared to have the tips of pine needles poking out the center of them.

Liz calmed herself, focused on being productive, rather than scared. She removed her backpack, laid it on the chair with a trembling hand.

"What are we going to do? What *can* we do?" Iggy asked not knowing Liz's plan and stared helplessly at her father.

She didn't answer. Iggy heard the sound of her unzipping the backpack. Suddenly, he could smell it - Forevergreen. The misty cloud of perfume fell all around him, filled his nostrils, awakened his mind.

He turned to find Liz holding the bottle with hope in her eyes. He raised his eyebrows.

Okay, he said without words. *Let's do this.*

Chapter 15

Friday – 8:08 am

Before the bell that would start first period, Liz sauntered up and down the aisles of desks, to where Mike sat. She sprayed a small cloud from her perfume bottle over Mike. The bottle she had found in the basement. Not fully understanding what she was up to, he trusted her, knowing whatever she was doing must have been important.

She moved to the next desk, spraying as she walked. Some of the kids didn't even notice; others complained, but she continued and ended at Jade in the back corner.

Jade's curious eyes asked questions; Liz winked at her. *Trust me.*

Mr. Miller's voice cracked throughout roll call. His watery eyes kept tabs on Liz, as he began teaching the day's lesson on sentence structure and punctuation. Beads of sweat formed on his brow, and his legs wobbled when walking from his chair to the blackboard. He acted ill, weak.

The majority of the class didn't seem to take notice, but Liz, Iggy, Jade, and Mike watched him closely, studied his twitching and coughing.

"I'm going to need a volunteer to come up and add the proper punctuation to this sentence," the teacher said, struggling to project his weakening voice.

Liz discreetly pumped a couple of squirts from the perfume bottle onto her neck and raised her hand. Mr. Miller looked at her, then scanned the room for another willing student. Any other willing student. Without him even calling on her, Liz made her way to the front of the room.

With his back against the chalkboard, he handed her the dusty, white stick of chalk. Even though he held his breath, he could still feel it. The whites of his eyes were gone, colored a deep red. Blood red.

It frightened Liz, but she refused to look away

from his painful stare. He trembled. All that was keeping him from falling down was his back pressing against the wall.

The stick of chalk slipped from the grip of Liz's fingers and hit the floor, breaking into bits. She put a few worried feet of space between herself and Mr. Miller when she noticed something start to press against the teacher's cheek from underneath the flesh. It pressed outward, then retracted then pressed out again. It pulsated, moving further out each time than the time before, seeming to gain strength with each push.

Mr. Miller's chest heaved, his breathing became problematic, irregular. The class began to take notice, but remained still in their seats. Iggy watched as Liz pulled the bottle of Forevergreen from her pocket, held it out in front of her, pointed at the teacher.

The pupils of his eyes shrank into small dots, turned the deepest shade of green Liz had ever seen. Mr. Miller mumbled something when she pressed down, sending a cloud of perfume at him.

When it landed on his skin, Liz jumped back a

few steps. His body held an electrical current, and he sputtered, gyrated, erratically.

The skin on his cheek finally gave way to the pressure and a long, green pine needle burst through. Blood spattered on Liz's shirt, and the classroom erupted in a frenzy screaming and pointing.

Mr. Miller stumbled to his knees then slowly gathered the energy to stand. He covered his cheek with his palm, hoping to hide the terrible sight.

"I'm not feeling well," he uttered, "I'll be back shortly. Read section four, until I return!"

He surged out of the door into the empty hallway, falling down several times before finally crawling into the teacher's lounge.

Iggy, Liz, Jade, and Mike gave a glance then bolted out behind him.

The trail of pine needles on the floor led them to the desperate teacher. Soon they could hear it. Painful screams filled their ears when they reached the closed door of the teacher's lounge. They peaked their four sets of eyes through the small window in the thick, wooden door and watched. It was happening.

Mr. Miller's body contorted, bent in ways it shouldn't be able to. His elbows strained backwards, disconnected from the joints. His legs wrapped around each other; his feet turned the wrong direction. His clothing shredded as long, prickly branches protruded through the fabric from his stomach and back.

His thighs expanded, ripping his pants, as more branches grew from his legs. His mouth opened wide, head tilted back, the top portion of a pine tree jolted out of it, growing until it reached the ceiling. His screaming faded, his body peeled away, falling lifeless to the floor. His shoes exploded as his toes grew long, firm, and cracked the floor as they penetrated far beneath it.

The transformation appeared to be over, as the kids stepped back from the window and silently formed a circle, all facing one another. In the teacher's lounge stood a pine tree, an evergreen, roots firmly growing into the floor, branches covered completely with needles.

Mr. Miller was no more.

"How did you trigger that? What happened?"

asked Mike, shaking from what they had just witnessed.

"It's the perfume," Liz said, gleefully. "My mother always wore this. She used to make it in the garage. This is what they were writing about in the notebook."

"Is it magical?" Jade asked, grabbing the bottle from Liz and inspecting it closely.

"We don't know for sure," Iggy started to speculate, "It could be a chemical reaction, an allergic reaction of sorts. Whatever it is, you saw what it can do."

"Wow," Jade whispered in awe. She looked at Mike. "This could work. This could be the answer."

Mike silently agreed.

Liz and Iggy scanned the hallway. Strangely, no police stood guard or wandered the halls today. No one kept watch. Perhaps what happened to Liz's father had the department rethinking their strategy.

"How much do we know about it? What all is it capable of doing?" Mike wondered, excited the Forevergreen could put a stop to all of this.

"Well, we know that it keeps them away. They

can't stand it," Iggy said. "And apparently, when it's sprayed directly on them, they change."

"My mom and Giuseppe's notes said if they change when they are not in the forest," Liz started.

"It's permanent." Jade finished her sentence.

Mike jumped in, "They remain as evergreens."

"Forever green," Iggy pointed out.

"How many bottles do we have?" asked Jade.

"You and I will keep that one," Liz said, about the larger bottle she found in her mother's things.

"Iggy and Mike will take this one." She handed Iggy the second bottle. The small vial she had kept in her room for a year now. Her mother had given it to her, days before she became ill. There was very little of the potion remaining inside both bottles.

"This is all we have?" Mike worried.

"This is it. Two bottles, neither full," Iggy promptly confirmed.

The bell rang. Time for second period.

"Spray the kids in your next class," Liz ordered the two boys. "We'll do the same. When the time is right, spray Mr. Armstrong. But don't act too fast. If he senses it coming, he could make it to the pines before he changes. They'll be strong in the forest. We need them to change *before* they get there."

The boys nodded, understanding exactly what needed to be done.

*

Snowflakes fell gently outside of Ms. Cain's classroom, creating an ironically peaceful scene. Jade and Liz didn't share the amusement that the rest of the class did when they saw the fluffy flakes descending from the clouds. All of the students huddled around the windows, watching the snow fall, their backs to the teacher.

Jade and Liz sat, shoulders high, at their desks.

Ms. Cain took little notice of the snow or of the kids gathered at the windows. Her usual complacent demeanor, however, seemed gone, replaced instead with visible contempt. Her breathing was slow, her eyes straight forward, moving left and right from Jade to Liz, repeatedly.

Covered in the scent, the girls knew she wouldn't come near them, but it was obvious she sensed something dire. Jade stood up, Ms. Cain shuddered.

"What are you doing? Don't come near me," she pleaded, glancing at the door.

Liz jumped from her seat, ran over to the door, planting herself firmly in front of it. Ms. Cain's eyes began to turn red. Jade wandered over to the group of students, hearing them carry on.

"I can't believe it's snowing!"

"It's still September!"

"Wow! This is so amazing!"

"It's really coming down!"

"Look at the ground! It's covered with snow!"

Jade sprayed a curtain of Forevergreen over them. So enthused by the weather, they hardly noticed the fresh smelling haze falling around them.

Ms. Cain slowly raised her right hand, held it in front of her face. Liz winced at the sight. The yogurt loving teacher's hand had changed from plump and pasty to ridged and green.

Her fingers were like evergreen branches, hundreds of pine needles had sprouted from them. She swiftly hid her botanical digits under the desk and eyeballed Liz at the doorway, watching her, calculating an escape. Pupils shrinking, cheeks pulsating, Ms. Cain hopped up, plunging herself at the girl.

"Jade!" screamed Liz, as the heavy woman thumped towards her with rage.

Jade saw Liz, helpless in front of the of thunderous thighs steamrolling at her. Instinctively, she threw the bottle of Forevergreen from where she stood, across the room, to Liz.

The trajectory of her underhand toss was like a rainbow, shooting from the ground through the bright sky to a marvelous pot of gold on the opposite end. It spun, just grazing the ceiling tiles, before descending a perfect arc into Liz's hands, arriving just before Ms. Cain collided with her.

In a fluent motion, Liz caught, aimed, and fired the perfume, forming a wall of scent between herself and the charging teacher.

The woman plowed through it, now with pine needles jutting from her face, her skin boiled instantly from its touch.

Liz sidestepped just in time to avoid a collision with the hideous monster, as it ran through the open door into the hallway.

Ms. Cain's body smashed, face first, onto the hard, wax coated floor. She flailed, as Liz and Jade watch from just inside the classroom. Pine needle covered branches ripped through her body from inside. She didn't scream or cry, but her face contorted quietly from the pain.

Her beady eyes stared back at the girls, silently cursing them, as air from her lungs wheezed out of her mouth. She flipped over and a large, thick branch grew from her stomach, splitting her torso wide open. Defying gravity, her body lifted off the dirty floor, pivoting on her heels, upright and tall.

Her eyes were frozen open, blankly staring, as branches cultivated from her face, neck, and skull. The portions of her skin still exposed, leached sticky sap from every pore. Her legs turned firm, ragged, forming into bark, and roots grew out of her feet and drilled themselves into the crumbling floor.

She stretched, pushing through the ceiling, as a shower of pine needles rained down around her.

A few more violent shakes and it was over. Ms. Cain was gone.

What had been the girls' study hall teacher was now a firmly rooted pine tree, punching through the ceiling of the two-hundred hallway.

*

Iggy and Mike tried desperately to participate in warmups without blowing their cover. Mr. Armstrong seemed unaware that Mr. Miller had fully transformed outside of the forest. The bottle of Forevergreen rolled around loosely in the pocket of Iggy's sweatpants. As they sat down to do curl-ups, he could hear the glass bottle clanging against the hardwood.

Clink.

Mike noticed it, too, but no one else seemed to pay any attention. Instead, they all listened to Mr. Armstrong count. *One, two, three. One, two, three.*

The two undercover allies waited, patiently, for their moment, both wondering how Liz and Jade had fared in Ms. Cain's class. If they only knew what was about to happen to Mr. Armstrong when they doused him with the perfume...

"Okay! Bring it in!" the teacher yelled, motioning with his hand for the kids to gather around him. "Seeing how it's snowing out. Yeah, that's right, it's snowing out. We once again will not be outside starting our baseball portion of Physical Education."

Whispers about the snow started to build to a crescendo. There were no windows in the gymnasium, so none of the boys could see the flurries falling.

"I know, I know," Mr. Armstrong said, signaling with his hands to be quiet. "That means dodgeball!"

All the whispers about snow dramatically ceased, replaced with whispers about Iggy and Mike. All the kids had witnessed the fight that happened yesterday during dodgeball and could hardly hold in the excitement of anticipating it might possibly happen again.

"Now," Mr. Armstrong said, one index finger pointed at Iggy, the other at Mike, "Let's see if these two stud muffins can keep it under control today." Malice shot from his stern glare at each of them. "I am not breaking up a wrestling match today. Understood?"

The class was silent, Iggy and Mike nodded in agreement.

"You will deeply regret a repeat performance of that nonsense." The teacher moved close to Iggy, caught a whiff of Forevergreen from his clothing. Mr. Armstrong sniffed, nearly gagged then made a grimace like he had swallowed a spoonful of glass.

Whatever he was going to say, he didn't. Instead he held his tongue, sensing that whatever he just inhaled was dangerous and harmful.

Taking a step back into less contaminated air, he hollered, "Line 'em up! Same teams as yesterday!"

The kids hustled to their respective sides of the

gym. Bouncing and skipping, they expected a battle for the ages, a massacre to ensue. Iggy and Mike walked, slowly, communicating without words, plotting something, hoping to find a spot to execute their mission.

Mr. Armstrong stepped between them, coughed, and covered his nose.

"Get to your spots, you two," he mumbled through his hand, with a nasally tone. "Don't test me today." He coughed again, a deep growl, until he finally gagged and walked away to place the balls on the center line.

Their steps stomping, cutting through the tranquil air, Iggy and Mike both were the last of their teams to line up on the back walls. All eyes studied them, watching the two stare each other down.

Iggy touched his thigh, feeling the bottle of fragrance still safely nestled in his pocket. All the players leaned in, waiting for the whistle, waiting to charge.

With all the students focused, the gym quieted to where Iggy and Mike could hear Mr. Armstrong's deep inhalation. Before he could exhale into his chrome whistle and send the high-pitched tone into the gym, both team captains bolted towards the middle of the court.

Like rogue steam engines on the same track, coursing towards collision, determined to derail the other, they sprinted. Stride for stride, they recklessly ignored Mr. Armstrong's waving arms and bellowing voice commanding that they stop.

The kids watched, jaws on the floor, eyes popped. A split second before impact, Iggy and Mike both veered slightly. Visually the crash was impressive, both of them falling violently to the ground. Physically, however, the damage was minimal, leaving them both unharmed.

Mr. Armstrong raced to the middle of the court, screaming obscenities, spitting with fury. Iggy thrusted his hand into the pocket of his Lakewood Pines Middle School printed sweatpants and stopped the bottle of perfume from rolling out.

Mike saw it and jumped on top of him to conceal it from Mr. Armstrong who arrived at that precise moment, grabbing Mike by the back of the neck, pulling him off Iggy.

Arms tightly folded, eyebrows furled, the gym teacher's foot tapped gently. Fire built through him, burning his chest, throat. With white knuckles he gripped his own biceps, seething with anger.

*

The weather had finally started to turn, the experiment with Sissy Daniels had been a success, and all things were going his way, until now. He studied what used to be his faithful follower, Mr. Miller, what was left of him anyway. The strong wooden stalk was deeply rooted in the floor, the top of the tree disappeared into the ceiling.

How could it be? Sheila and Giuseppe had both been dealt with. Chief Jackson, the last human he believed could possibly interfere with his plan had also been taken care of. He grinned slightly, feeling confident despite this small, inconvenient set back.

A bump in the road, he thought.

I am too powerful to stop, he reassured himself. With the permanent winter taking shape and his perfected procedure to procure an army of loyal servants working great, he feared nothing. What could foil this? Who could get in the way? *No one.*

Principal Warren turned and exited the teacher's lounge, leaving Mr. Miller there, dripping sap and dropping pine needles.

*

As they squeaked between the lockers and the tips of the branches that had grown from Ms. Cain, one branch had enough tree sap on it to grab hold of Liz's sweater. The sticky twig pulled a string of fabric loose, as she sucked in her belly to keep herself away from it.

"This situation has gotten a bit sticky," Jade said, pulling her belly in to avoid contacting the tree.

Liz used her fingertips to pry the prickly branch off herself, leaving a thread of her knitted top in its grasp when it finally pulled free.

"Gross," she said, shaking her hand, flinging the few needles that were stuck to her skin. "I always thought

Ms. Cain needed to branch out a little and try some new things, but this is ridiculous."

They both flinched when the sound of expensive, leather shoes clicking on the floor came floating through the hall. The steps echoed just around the corner, moving rapidly towards them.

Liz and Jade darted, quickly into the girls restroom and held the door so that it closed gently, with almost no sound at all. The smiling image of Sissy Daniels taped to the inside of the door greeted them.

When the footsteps passed, Liz and Jade pushed the door slightly ajar and spied out through the small gap.

With mouth gaping in disbelief, Principal Warren stood stoic. Then he circled the tree, stroked the branches, and caressed them lightly. He orbited twice before stopping and running his fingers through his well styled hair. He nibbled his manicured nails, assessed his emotions, feeling despair.

She was his most dedicated follower, his confidant, his **beloved**. All through the planning, the experiments, the murders, she stood by him, supporting his agenda.

Why her? he thought. Whoever was responsible would pay, would feel the reign of his terror. Destruction would certainly find the people of Lakewood.

"What happened?" came a voice from behind him, followed by other exasperated phrases in different tones. He put on his caring, docile educator face, turned, and saw students from Ms. Cain's study hall gathering around.

He had perfected this charade over the years since being sent here to establish the race. To build a nation of monsters, creatures that could be used to rule over this planet's inhabitants. With one vicious swipe of his arm, he could have annihilated the entire group of the feeble-minded human offspring. But, he didn't. They were all the perfect size for planting, as his tests on Sissy Daniels had proven.

"Please, children, get back into the classroom and lock the door," he warned in an urgent but gentle voice. "It's dangerous out here. Stay inside until I come back for you." Panic flooded their eyes, but they listened to their principal.

Brats. He didn't need them getting in the way now. No doubt the ones that sent him here would be less than pleased that two of his helpers had been permanently transformed. The last thing he needed was more interference, more trouble, or to snap and wipeout some of his potential harvest.

What he needed to do was find Armstrong.

Armstrong could help him get to the bottom of this, contain the problem, and then get these rotten children to the pines for their first round of treatment. Warren would then be able to explain these few mishaps to the leaders when they came for him.

Plant the crops, send the Signal.

Plant the crops, send the Signal.

That was all that mattered now.

Chapter 16

Coughing, Mr. Armstrong shoved both Iggy and Mike onto a bench after dragging them by their shirt collars into the boys locker room. Struggling to catch his breath, he began to sternly scold, "Boys, I… I have… I have had..."

But, the Forevergreen on their clothes choked him. The riled teacher pulled his burning hands away and gritted his teeth. His wrinkled forehead glowed red; the muscles in his arms rippled with tension.

"I've had it! You boys are asking for it!" He reared back and slapped his boiled palm across Iggy's face.

The much smaller Iggy nearly fell back off the bench onto the grimy tiled floor. Mike blasted off from his seat on the wood bench to protect Iggy. With one arm, the teacher thrusted Mike back to the bench. The boy was helpless against Mr. Armstrong's power.

Armstrong bent down, nose to nose with Mike. A wicked laugh seeped from the depth of his belly.

"Do you think you can stop me from hurting him?" His voice sunk and lowered with each word. "You weaklings seem to enjoy fighting each other. You don't want to fight *me*? You scared?" He laughed again. His sweaty face housed gritted teeth and bloodshot eyes. Heat from his stale breath blasted against Mike's fluttering eyelids.

The snarl of his words was ethereal, frighteningly deep and coarse, engulfing the entire locker room. He grabbed one of them with each hand and tossed them against the lockers behind them. The sound of their bodies smashing against the metal doors harmonized with the sound of glass falling onto the grungy floor.

The floor had a slope from all angles, leading to a tiny, circular, brass colored drain, designed to remove water when the showers in the locker room spilled out. It also captured other items, like little, cylinder-shaped bottles of perfume.

Mike and Iggy both saw the glass tube of Forevergreen laying in the middle of the room, several feet from them with the angry teacher in the way of it. Luckily, Mr. Armstrong, in his fit of rage, didn't notice it there.

A low gurgle, a rumble from the pit of Mr. Armstrong's guts, creeped past his lips, haunting the atmosphere. His eyes burned with hatred and anger. He began to twist his upper body, left and right with such force, Iggy thought he might spin completely around from the waist up.

With one harsh jerk of his neck, a strong, bark covered pine tree branch burst out of Mr. Armstrong's shoulder, six feet in length. His body jolted again, this time a branch shot from his neck, tipping his head to the right. The gym teacher watched it grow from his body with the corner of his eye and knew what was happening.

He knew he was in the process of a permanent transformation. He needed get to the forest! With a hunched back, his legs wobbling, Mr. Armstrong fought for balance with each difficult step.

Reading the desperation on his face and sensing his vulnerability, the boys knew they had to stop this morphing creature from leaving the locker room and finding its way to the pines. Mike leaped to his feet, rushed at the monster, and grabbed hold of the branch growing from its back.

Yanking and pulling, Mike tried to hold Mr. Armstrong in place. Iggy seized his only chance, dove head first, sliding along the scum coated floor, right through the open legs of Mr. Armstrong. His momentum carried him clear to the drain and to the Forevergreen bottle. He snagged it and flipped over to face up at the beast.

Another branch erupted from its back, striking a blow to Mike's head, knocking free his grip. Iggy watched Mike fall hard to the floor then looked straight up.

I have a clear shot! Iggy thought determinedly.

From his back, Iggy reached his arm out, finger on the spray pump, and sent a shot of Forevergreen up at the hideous plant/human hybrid. The spray flowed gracefully up, two thin lines climbing into Armstrong's nostrils.

In an instant, silence filled the room. The monster seemed paralyzed, still, except for its eyes, slowly moving to look at Iggy.

As it peered into the boy's soul, Iggy could see the true horror inside of it. A being from the pits of hell, standing over him. An evil designed to destroy innocence, an entity created to bring pain. In a magnificent, spontaneous combination, the creature bellowed a deafening, ear-piercing scream, and hundreds of pine tree branches broke through its body, turning Mr. Armstrong instantly into a tall, full pine tree.

"Are you okay?" Mike called to Iggy from across the room through the thick branches of the enormous pine tree growing from the floor that separated them.

"I'm good. You?"

"Yeah, I'm good."

They sat up, both tarred and feathered with tree sap and pine needles from the debris. Fallout from the glorious explosion had left them covered in the chaotic aftermath. A few deep breaths of shared relief shuffled between them.

The pause for recovery, however, was brief. With only a moment to regain their strength, Iggy and Mike gasped as the locker room door creaked open. *Click. Click. Click.*

"Damn you," a hollow voice whispered hatefully.

With his face straight, pale, anguished--Principal Warren gave the startled boys a once over, expressionless. They watched him closely, monitoring his reaction to what he viewed before him. His body shuttered; a shiver of disgust rolled down his spine.

It was the last straw, the moment of truth. The plan, his purpose, deteriorated, crumbled through his fingertips. Principal Warren's chest wheezed, each breath a sign of his growing anger. Now, his General had been destroyed. The one who was to lead his army was now useless. All those years of experience accumulated through the wars and battles that their kind had fought was gone.

Mike slid across the floor, positioned himself

defensively next to Iggy.

"You two," the principal muttered softly yet beastly, "you are the ones. Mr. Miller, Ms. Cain. It was you."

"Whatever you're planning, whatever horrible thing you're trying to do, it won't work. We can stop it," Iggy stated, projecting a fearlessness that Mike admired from his side. The principal was too far away for Iggy to reach with a spray of Forevergreen.

"I assure you, my plan can still come to fruition," he promised, his intent dripping with evil. His face grew wicked and red.

"Whatever you did to them, how you turned them won't work on me. I am much stronger, much more resilient. Every student in this school will belong to me. My army will grow. I'll accomplish what they sent me here to do. Lakewood belongs to *me*."

Suddenly, Warren's eyes turned the deepest, darkest crimson. Iggy and Mike sat up, looked questioningly at each other. "Do you smell that?" Mike demanded.

Forevergreen! Floating through the air, over the head of Principal Warren, the light drizzle of evergreen scent settled on his hair and shoulders like a heavy morning fog.

When Warren spun around to peer behind him at the hallway door, Iggy and Mike could see them. Liz and Jade stood poised for combat! Liz held her arm proudly out in front of her, bottle in hand.

Principal Warren glowered at her, remembered watching her mother die. He thought of her father, lying in the hospital succumbing to the sickness, nearing death.

Smugly, he relished the thought of now killing *her*. One blow to her body and she'd never recover, never crack another smile, never take another breath.

All of them, those four pests. Those two delinquent misfits couldn't stop him. Neither could those two middle school soap opera stars. The drama king and queen themselves. The two love birds. Oh, he couldn't wait to see the look on Igor Andrews' face while he watched the sweet and innocent Elizabeth Jackson balled up on the floor gasping for air, as her young soul leaves her body.

And Mike, the troublemaker, the tough guy who won't look so cool when he was ripped in half, one end on either side of this room. Mike's parents would thank him for it, too. They never loved him, never wanted him anyway.

Then Jade. The quiet one. The one who did well in school, but put on the act of being a rebel. The phony. What use would she be to his army anyway? The weak one. Disposing of her ahead of time would only achieve the inevitable. Jade would never have lasted through the battle that lay ahead, as they took over this wretched human race and their planet.

And last Igor. The annoying one. A goodie-two-shoes who never really fit in. Not with the smart kids or with the jocks. He just puttered around, following Liz like a lost puppy with nowhere to call home. Warren smirked with delight when he remembered running Iggy's parents off the road, killing them instantly when their car ran head on into a tall and sturdy pine tree.

Liz and Jade shielded their eyes with their

forearms, seeing the rage of Principal Warren manifest into a balled fist. The empty bottle fell from Liz's hand and shattered. He reached back, ready to punish them with his unearthly might, when he suddenly cringed.

Arm raised, he froze before it could descend upon them and the demonic flair in his eye dissolved. Fear glazed over his face.

What was happening? Principal Warren's thoughts screamed.

He shook, his head spun side to side. A tall branch shot right up from the top of his skull. He fought it, kicked against it with wicked resolve. His insides burned fire; he could feel it embarking.

When this happened in the pines, he gained strength and power, became unstoppable. But here, out of the sacred pines of Lakewood, he'd be destroyed if he transformed. He'd face the same brutal, eternal demise as Miller, Cain, and Armstrong.

Principal Warren arrogantly thought, *Surely, I can still muster the power to wipe out these four senseless children before changing. But then what? I probably won't have enough time to make it to the pines before completing the transformation. So, I will deal with them later. Right now, I must run.*

Before his first step, another long branch extended from the middle of Principal Warren's back, almost grazing the end of Iggy's nose. Screaming in agony, pleading for the pain to stop, he crashed toward the door. The girls sidestepped when he burst his way past them.

Get to the pines, Principal Warren's mind cried out. *Get there now!*

He struggled into the lengthy corridor outside of the locker room and forced the long, awkward branches on his body through the first exit, leaving a pile of needles behind. Stumbling, he lurched across the snow covered schoolyard, to the baseball diamonds, towards the pines.

Every five or six steps he tumbled down, flat in the fluffy white powder. Up again, each time, he pressed on. Branches streamed out of him, from all over his body. His screams of agony intensified. Unable to stand, **near third base of the second ball field,** his body flopped like a freshly caught fish on the floor of the boat, desperate and helpless.

With impaired vision, he barely could see the blurry forest, waiting for him, ready to take him in. His salvation was close.

He crawled, wiggled his way, inch by inch, gaining hope.

Closer.

Closer.

Closer.

Chapter 17

Terrified, Liz rushed to Iggy, plowing her lips directly into his. Mike and Jade embraced desperately.

"Can you believe the sound it makes? When the branches come out of them?" Jade shook off the memory with a quiver.

"He was going to kill us," Liz said. "I'm sure of it. I could see it in his eyes."

Iggy exhaled, relieved, "We're safe now." He held Liz closer.

"We're not out of the woods yet," said Mike. He turned and opened one of the lockers, grabbed a Lakewood Pines hoodie and sweatpants, tossed them to Liz.

"Here, put these in your backpack. We need to get

out there." He and Jade rushed to the hallway, Iggy and Liz anxiously followed. Mike opened a rusty, blue door that read *Maintenance* near the exit that Warren used, pulled out two shovels. Not snow shovels, but digging ones. Heavy and pointed.

"What's this for?" asked Iggy, as Mike handed one to him, keeping the other for himself.

"Look," Mike pointed through the glass window at the pines. Warren's struggle had left a long trail in the fresh snow, leading directly to where he entered the forest.

"He's in the forest. He made it. If we don't hurry, she will be gone forever."

Stepping out into the whiteness, wind and flakes blasted their cheeks. They trudged through the deep snow; bright green needles carpeted Principal Warren's snaking path.

The brewing storm, quickly intensified, no doubt fueled by the wicked strength Principal Warren gathered in the pines. The wind, harsh and cold, made verbal communication difficult. But the foursome didn't need to speak; they were feeling the same: scared but ready.

There was no telling just how powerful Principal Warren would be now that he was in the pines. The evil place where all his energy originated, where all his destructiveness swarmed.

Visibility worsened as the wind and falling flakes buried the trail, but, determined, Mike led them. He remembered precisely the location of the shimmering, small tree deep in the pines.

Carefully, Iggy pushed back the low branches on the trees as they entered the pines. Small, dried, and fragile--several twigs broke off at the slightest touch. He wished that Principal Warren could be so easily damaged, but he knew better.

Ironically, the trees brought some safety and relief from the blistering cold. The wind couldn't touch the team once inside the pines, and the snow hadn't reached the forest floor through the dense canopy of thick pine branches clinging together overhead.

Liz stared up, realizing how strong all the tall, healthy pines were when they worked together. That's what the four of them needed to be: *together*. One pine tree standing in the middle of a field was vulnerable and timid. Right now, the kids knew they needed to surpass the strengthening unity of the forest.

Liz and Jade struggled to weave through the entwined branches, and the boys labored to duck below the jabbing needles of the closely positioned trees. With some sections more open than others, the kids jostled back and forth, searching for the safest path.

Winter skylight faintly lit the undergrowth, and the deep forest shadowed their vision. When Mike stopped, they all understood why. Light had broken through the massive pine trees, streaming down in beams, and bright white snowflakes trickled in and out of them, like fairies dancing and twirling.

Encased in the rays of sunlight, it patiently waited for them. It stood silently, anxious to see them. Its branches, small but firm, daringly reached out to them.

"It is taller than a few days ago when Iggy and I first saw it that morning before school," Liz informed Jade. They stared, all of them mesmerized by its peaceful glow beneath the much taller pines.

"Spray it," Mike said to Liz, handing her his bottle with the last few drops of Forevergreen puddled in the bottom.

She didn't question his idea. She slid the backpack off her shoulder and rested it on the ground by her feet. Taking a breath nervously, Liz walked in a circle around it, spraying all its branches. They watched, not even sure what they should be expecting to see, what type of reaction would ensue.

In the quiet, among their fearful panting, it moved. The small pine tree shuddered, slightly. They jumped back, afraid but excited. They waited for it to move again, but it didn't.

"Come on," Iggy demanded, not looking away from the alone tree. "We brought these for a reason."

He slowly walked towards the tree, pushed the end of his shovel into the soil, pressed on the edge of it with his foot, sinking it deep. He scooped out a chunk of dirt, tossed it aside. The little tree wiggled again.

Jade flinched. "It's working," she whispered, amazed. "Mike, go," she ordered, motioning ahead, while taking a step back. She gave Mike a gentle shove to his shoulder, pushing him forward.

He gulped and joined Iggy.

Together, with Liz and Jade watching from a distance, the boys dug scoop after scoop from the ground. The tree shook and squirmed with each scoop of dirt they removed. Soon the snow that had glazed each needle had been knocked free and fallen to the ground. Mike's shovel nicked the base of the tree trunk, chipping a piece of bark away. One of the branches reached out and whacked Mike on the shoulder.

With a snorting laugh, Iggy blurted, "She got you back!" Breath billowed from his mouth in the cold air like a buff of a train engine. The girls, equally amused, giggled and smiled. The light moment of silliness halted abruptly, suddenly. A howl, a growl, the demon sound, a screaming from deep in the pines sent an alarming chill through all of them.

Frightened and panicked, Liz tugged on Jade's shirt. "Come on, let's finish this so we can get out of here." She walked up and gently clutched a branch in each of her hands. The needles poked her cold skin, but she bit her lip and squeezed tighter.

"Guys, grab hold. Let's get her out."

When another terrible groan from Principal Warren rumbled through the trees, they rushed to help Liz. All four of them huddled close to find a place to fit their hands and grip the tree.

"Just hold on!" Liz yelled. "This might hurt, but we will be quick!"

Straining, they pulled but their footing wasn't solid, and their efforts were uneven.

"We have to pull together. At the same time!" Iggy yelled to be heard over the treacherous moans that inched closer to them. "On three, we give it all we've got! One. Two. Three!"

They yanked, huffing and gasping.

"Again!" Iggy commanded them. "One. Two. Three!"

They grunted and gritted their teeth and felt the roots start to pop under the tree.

"Again! One. Two. Three!"

James Alan Ross

They jerked fiercely, letting out loud groans of exhaustion. The tree gave a little, pulled up slightly from the dirt. Focused mightily on uprooting the tree, each of them kept an ear open to the upsurge building signaling Principal Warren's impending arrival.

This time, in unison, they all counted. "One. Two. Three!"

Their faces contorted from the exhausting effort. Every ounce of strength, every piece of their being pulled with relentless perseverance. They yelled loudly, hoping it would give them just a bit more power. Harder and harder they heaved, feet pressing firmly, backs leaning, arms stretched. **Suddenly with a squeal and bounce,** it gave way.

The roots jolted loose and released from the stubborn earth. They all fell back, tumbling down, crashing into a pile onto the snow covered ground. Catching their breath, they laid there, piled high like **a bad game** of Twister: Iggy and Mike on the bottom, Jade and Liz mangled and intertwined on top of them.

Their hearts and breathing completely froze when

242

they heard it.

"Thank you."

The voice that none of them knew softly trickled over them. The small pine tree they had pulled out was not on top of the human pile. Instead, covering them, draped over Liz and Jade was a girl--cold, scared, and wearing only a thin, torn nightgown.

They had never heard her speak before, but they knew that face. She had been staring at them everywhere they had been for the last week.

Sissy Daniels.

Chapter 18

Jade slammed one of her palms over each of Iggy's and Mike's eyes. "Lizard, your backpack!"

Liz rolled off the heap of tangled arms and legs and unzipped her bag. She grabbed the sweat suit out and urgently helped Sissy get the clothes on, covering up her ragged, intimate garments.

The four tired, Lakewood Middle School seventh-graders studied the girl from the *MISSING* posters. She was real. On the printed images, she was flat, posed. Here, her cheeks were round, her chin pointed, and her eyes moved like oversized, wet, glass marbles. The group studied her dark hair and caramel skin. She was thinner, shorter than the picture depicted. Her teeth chattered behind purple, cracked lips.

"I'm freezing," said the freed girl, dazed and wobbly. "Where are my parents?"

"We'll get you to them soon," Liz told Sissy. She rushed over and rubbed her hands rapidly up and down Sissy's arms to warm her. "Everyone, give me your socks."

The branches overhead rustled, Principal Warren's grumblings echoed loudly through the shaking trees. He was close. "Hurry!" She yelled. "Now!"

They broke their stare and untied their laces, pulled their shoes off, removed their socks, and handed them to Liz, before putting their shoes back on. She quickly slid them onto Sissy's blue feet, layer by layer until all four pairs were on, helping to warm her. No longer missing, she shivered, disoriented, not sure what had even happened to her.

Confused, she didn't fully understand. "It's snowing. How long have I been away?"

"A week," said Jade, blowing into her cupped hands. "Almost."

Sissy looked around. "But, it's so cold. It's

winter."

Warren's devilish roar rocked the branches above them sending needles down like the sudden rain shower that ruins a picnic.

"We can explain later. We're all just glad you're okay," Iggy told her glancing quickly over his shoulder to see if Principal Warren was in sight. He turned the other direction but, thankfully, still couldn't see him. Yet.

Sissy blindly trusted the group, just glad to be whole again. Glad to be human again. "That sound," she said scouring the forest with alertness. "Is that who did this to me?"

"Yes," Mike nodded, fearfully. "That's him. We need to get out of here. Get some help."

"Who could possibly help us?" replied Jade, hopelessly.

"Anyone! Anyone at all!" Mike responded back.

"Yeah, let's get out of these trees before it's too late," Iggy said, turning to lead the charge back to the school. But instead of taking a step, he lost his balance and fell to the ground, awkwardly.

The others turned to see him on his butt, knees bent, feet flatly planted in the ground. *Literally planted!* His feet were growing right into the dirt! When the rest of the group looked down, they could see that they too were trapped by roots, plunging deep into the soil.

Mike's arm was long enough to reach Iggy and help him stand upright. They all struggled desperately, attempting to free themselves, except Sissy. She just stood, her face in her hands, sobbing.

"It's no use!" she cried, hopelessly. "You'll never get free!" Just rescued, she couldn't bare the idea of transforming again.

The kids screamed for help, fully understanding that no one was there to hear them. Every tree in the forest shook, violently vibrating and convulsing. Pine needles fell like confetti on New Year's Eve in Times Square. The powerful roots of the pines rumbled under the ground, creating a magnificent earthquake. The dirt moved like whitecap waves in the ocean.

The desperate middle schoolers locked hands with each other, keeping themselves from falling, as they clung to the last bit of hope. The forest agitation didn't last more than a second. The trees bent down, opening a wide glade in the center of the pines.

Through the clearing came Principal Warren. He was no longer the Head Educator they once knew. Three times his normal height, entirely made of pine tree branches, he wore the face of a beast straight from the depths of Hades. His eyes ignited with fire, his teeth glistened sharp and jagged, his mouth widened to devour them. Flames burned from his lips, and a hideous smile formed like a striking cobra.

He had trapped the kids. These remaining threats were about to be destroyed, and Warren loved it. His plan had shockingly twisted, but still, he managed to succeed. His leaders, the elders waiting afar, would be pleased. They'd have to be. Once Warren could send the Signal, they'd come and congratulate him, anoint him with gratitude and recognition for fulfilling his duty and completing his earthly task.

The principal's grunting turned to an evil laugh of satisfaction, while he watched his students fight desperately for freedom. Liz couldn't reach her backpack, which she removed to help Sissy get dressed. Even if she could have, the Forevergreen was gone.

He tipped his large head back and opened his mouth wide. A beam of red fire exploded from his insides and towered high into the gray sky. He was sending the Signal. And when his leaders received it, when they arrived, all of humanity would face a war that it could not win.

And the war would start right there in the once peaceful Village of Lakewood. Every child on earth would be planted into the soil to grow into unsightly monsters loyal to the army and its cause of terror and domination.

Hysterical, Iggy Andrews, Liz Jackson, Mike Lawman, Jade Wilson, and Sissy Daniels held hands and waited. Accepting their demise, they watched the stream of flame shoot from the monster's throat high into the sky… Then it happened.

Silence.

The fire stopped. The trees and ground

stilled. Warren's body jerked, his face grew weary and pale. He jerked again, this time falling to one knee, as his left leg--wooden and bark covered--dropped from his body.

He roared, as his other leg cracked and tipped over, sending his helpless frame to the ground. Standing there, in the falling snow, the kids saw him: Chief Jackson, dressed in a hospital gown, wielding an axe. An axe that read, *Happy Birthday, Sweetheart* on the handle.

Chief Jackson climbed onto Warren's back and began to chop. Swing after swing, he severed branches from its body, remembering his wife's tears. He took bit by bit, slamming the axe head over and over into the wooden beast. Chards of sappy pine splintered about with every blow the chief landed.

Sheila knew, he thought while fighting off a flood of emotion. All that time, she knew. Needles stuck to his sweaty forehead and cheeks as he thrusted the axe again. Then again! Then again!

The kids watched him continue to chop, though it was clear that Principal Warren, the monster, was dead.

Jackson paused and looked at the group of heroes standing before him. His eyes stopped on his daughter's, and he could have sworn he was looking at Sheila.

Finding the final drop of energy in the tank he raised his arms, axe firmly squeezed between his calloused hands. With a primitive howl he brought the blade crashing down, jamming it deep into the broken and cut up pine tree. A sigh of relief drifted from his lungs and his head and shoulders dropped emphatically.

Calmly, almost unnoticeably, the air warmed, the clouds faded away, and the snow quietly melted into puddles on the needle-covered ground. As the wood chips had flown off the end of the blade, piling high, the kids loosened from the roots and soil. Liz opened her arms wide and instinctively they all embraced, squeezing and bouncing with glee.

With one final swing, the Lakewood Chief of Police sunk the axe deep into the back of the monster's head and left it stuck there. He hobbled down off the mound of wood pieces, still weak from his illness. Liz wrapped her arms around his belly, holding tight, thankful her father was alive.

"Mom knew, Dad!" she said, face buried into her father's chest.

"Yeah, Honey. Mom knew," he said, softly, and kissed the top of her head.

"We are so happy to see you, Mr. Jackson," Iggy exclaimed, running up to them. The rest of the gang followed quickly behind.

Jackson's face turned to an expression of gratitude. He held his hand out. "Iggy, I owe you an apology. Mike, you too."

Both young men gave the chief a firm, respectable handshake.

"You both did a fantastic job. I'm proud of you," he told them. "Jade, you were equally amazing."

The shy girl smiled at him.

He went on, "This morning when Liz and Iggy sprayed me with Forevergreen, they told me everything that you all had been up to. They didn't know I could hear them, but I could. Every single word."

He turned and focused on the new girl. With a

smile and a playful point, he said, "I think someone has been looking for you."

They all laughed at his understatement.

"Let's get you home, Sissy Daniels," he said, wiping needles from his face and brushing them off his hospital gown.

As they walked out together, Liz took her hand and wrapped it tightly around Iggy's. He looked at her, happy she was okay, happy she still loved him.

It had always been *her*. *Always.*

Chapter 19

One year later…

Squinting from the brightly shining sun, Mike's arms were growing numb. "Got it!" he celebrated, as Jade clapped from the sidewalk below. He steadily made his way down the wooden ladder, then stood, side by side, with the girl who had his heart.

"It looks phenomenal," she declared, grinning ear to ear.

The new sign was in position. *Sheila's Place: Home of the Original Greasy's Pizza.*

"Nice work, you two," Chief Jackson said, walking outside, wiping wet paint from his fingers. "We'll be ready to open before you know it."

"Buying Greasy's was a great idea. It's an important place to all of us," Mike told him, glad to be on the chief's good side.

"Yeah, well, don't forget our deal. I'm going to need help from all of you if we're going to really make a-go of it," the man who heroically chopped the evergreen monster into pieces reminded them with raised eyebrows.

"Dad! Guys!" Liz called, sticking her head through the front door from inside. "We've got something to show you." She motioned with her hand for them follow then ran back inside the shop.

The three of them went into the pizza shop to see what Liz and Iggy had to share with them. The smell of sawdust and sheetrock from the remodeling job was strong, but the smell of cheese, tomato sauce, and pepperoni was stronger. Iggy stood, clammy and tired beside Liz, whose face was streaked with flour and sweat. In front of them, on the new stainless-steel counter top was a thin, round, extra-large pizza from the oven.

"We've done it," announced Iggy. "At least, I think we have," he said with less confidence.

"Well, it took five tries, but we think we have finally nailed Giuseppe's secret recipe," Liz explained, rapidly. "First our crust was too thick. Then our sauce was too runny. Then not enough cheese."

"Is it greasy?" her dad asked, leaning in and visually inspecting the pie.

She exhaled, nodded with assuredness.

The chief's eyes raised to Iggy. "Stain your car seats greasy?"

Mike pushed his way past Jackson. "There's only one way to find out for sure." He pulled a slice from the round, sloppy mess. The cheese stretched out from the center to his mouth, never breaking. As he bit down, the counter below caught a puddle of slimy grease that dripped from the gooey triangle.

"Well?" Jade wondered with anticipation. "How is it?" She bounced up and down unable to handle the suspense.

Mike chewed, thoroughly and swallowed. He pondered the taste, the consistency. All eyes were on him, begging for the verdict.

"Come on, Mike," Iggy pleaded, quietly. "How is it?"

"Giuseppe would be proud," Mike stated, sentimental and sappy.

"All right!" the new shop owner cheered, quickly being joined in celebration by the four kids.

Peace had once again found the Village of Lakewood, Lakewood Pines Middle School, and now, finally, Greasy's Pizza Shop. Normalcy had settled over Lakewood. People fell back into their routines and, although they'd never be forgotten, the tragic events surrounding the disappearance of Sissy Daniels slowly faded into the past. Replicating the pizza that Giuseppe had been selling at Greasy's for years smack in the middle of the village was the final piece of the puzzle.

All feeling the excitement, Chief Jackson, Iggy, Liz, and Jade grabbed a slice and joined Mike in devouring it. With mozzarella stuck to their chins and grease coating their fingers, the gang exchanged looks of happiness with bloated cheeks and chomping jaws.

Then, they stopped chewing. One by one, with big eyes, they glanced at the others, knowing exactly what was poking their gums and the roofs of their mouths. The silence filling the room felt thick and heavy. No one dared to speak. No one wanted it to be true.

Iggy pushed the chewed pizza around inside his mouth with his tongue. Slowly, he reached his hand up, took a single finger, and slid it between his lips. As he held his breath, his friends silently watch him pull from his mouth a long, green pine needle.

The End

94280424R00159

Made in the USA
Columbia, SC
24 April 2018